THE COUNCIL OF NICAEA A.D. 325

A HISTORICAL NOVEL
WHEN CRISIS THREATENED
THE EARLY CHRISTIAN CHURCH

E.D.S. SMITH

OUTSKIRTS PRESS
DENVER, COLORADO

The Council of Nicaea A.D. 325
A Historical Novel - When Crisis Threatened The Early Christian Church
All Rights Reserved.
Copyright © 2015 E.D.S. Smith
v3.0 r1.0

Outskirts Press, Inc.
http://www.outskirtspress.com

ISBN: 978-1-4787-3942-5

Outskirts Press and the "OP" logo are trademarks belonging to Outskirts Press, Inc.

PRINTED IN THE UNITED STATES OF AMERICA

I dedicate this book to my four children, with all love.

Introduction

The Council of Nicaea, modern day Turkey, was convened in A.D. 325 by Emperor Constantine, sole ruler of the Roman Empire. Close to 300 bishops from the empire came to Nicaea to standardize some of the Christian Church's practices, but most importantly, to settle a theological controversy among the bishops that was weakening and threatening the stability of the Roman Empire: Was Jesus Christ the Only Begotten Son of God, Equal to God, and true God from true God, or was he subordinate and inferior to God the Father as preached by a priest named Arius. Both sides had followers, and the arguments, even street fights between clergy and lay people on opposing sides, caused Constantine great concern that the unity and the stability of the empire was at risk.

Christians have been in Rome and elsewhere since Jesus' time, but it was not until the Edict of Milan in A.D. 313 that ended Christian persecution and gave Christians freedom of religion with same rights and privileges as the pagans. But almost since the beginning of Christianity, conflicts and theological heresies emerged, necessitating Church fathers to convene councils and settle disputes. The Council of Nicaea, often called the Great Council, condemned the Arian controversy, and established that Jesus was Divine by Nature, the Only Begotten Son of God the Father, and true God from true God. The attending bishops adopted a creed know as the Nicene Creed, affirming and establishing Jesus' Divinity.

This is also a love story happening at the time of the Council, and includes Rome, Nicaea and places in between. Emperor Constantine, his sister Constantia, the priest Arius, and several named Roman emperors and unnamed bishops were real people, but other characters are fictitious. Constantine himself described his vision of Christ on the eve of the Battle of the Milvian Bridge in A.D. 312, who told him to fight under the sign of the cross and he will be victorious. His adoption of Christianity after his victory, and the affirmation at the Council of Nicaea in A.D. 325 that Jesus was Divine, changed world history.

Chapter 1

Night of October 27, A.D. 312
Constantine's Camp outside Rome on the Eve
of the Battle of the Milvian Bridge

Constantine, Caesar Augustus of the Western Roman Empire jumped from his bed and grabbed his sword which lay by his pillow. Something roused him from his sleep but he wasn't sure what it was. His eyes darted from right to left, his body stood on alert as he listened for sounds of assassins. Outside the tent his loyal troops stood at attention allowing no one to enter, yet he dared not underestimate the possibility of a traitor among them.

In the corner hung his freshly polished armor and the purple plumed helmet indicating his imperial rank. His shield bearing a gold eagle with wings spread in a posture of flight was propped by the side. The royal standard with a golden eagle as Caesar Augustus of the Western Empire stood by his bed. On the other side of the tent on a gold pedestal was a statue of the sun god Mithras killing a bull, the soldiers' god of victory.

He had camped on the outskirts of Rome on the eve of this final battle to conquer the city and become the supreme ruler of the Western Empire. As he marched south from Gaul defeating town after town along the Italian peninsula, he had left them intact, ordering his troops not to plunder or kill the citizens. As word spread of his benevolence, towns along the way surrendered and opened their gates to him. When he reached the gates of Rome his troops had been jubilant, his commanders confident of the final victory. But he had misgivings. Will he, in this final battle for the supremacy of the Western Empire perish at the hand of his enemy Maxentius, the emperor of Rome? Will his head be mounted on a pike as his enemy marched in triumph to the elated cries of the Roman citizens lining the streets?

He had already prayed and sacrificed to Mithras as well as to Mars the god of war, and Jupiter the god of all gods, and ordered his troops to do the same. But it was Mithras who had given him victory after victory and who held a special place in his soldiers' hearts. He hoped that Mithras would look favorably at him once more and give him Rome.

Satisfied at not finding anything unusual in his tent and believing that his mind played tricks on him, Constantine lay down his sword and stretched out on his bed, wishing for a few hours of sleep before the battle. In spite of his foreboding and doubts he drifted into a deep sleep.

Suddenly a brilliant light shone in his eyes. The rays were intense and blinding, gushing from a blazing cross. In front of the cross immersed in the golden beams stood a man in a white robe, his arms extended in a gesture of welcome. Gazing at the image Constantine was not afraid, only curious.

The man's look was stern and commanding, yet his features were soft and his demeanor humble. A warm feeling overtook Constantine. There was something special about the man. He was different from anyone he had seen before.

"Who are you?" Constantine asked reaching for his sword out of habit.

"Put down your sword Constantine, for it will not protect you should I wish it. I am Jesus Christ, the God of the Christians. I came to you with a message. The empire has been persecuting my followers and I want that to stop."

The words stunned Constantine and for a moment he could not speak. Finding his voice he said, "Sir, I have not been persecuting your followers and neither had my father when he ruled the Western Empire. I have Christians in my service, my close advisor is Christian, and some of my soldiers are Christians."

"I know that. You have been tolerant of the Christians but that's not enough for me. You have not yet embraced me as your God."

"It is true I haven't embraced you but I am open to your teachings."

"I want more than that. I want you to shed your pagan gods and accept me as the one and only true God. I want you to be the Roman Empire's first Christian emperor."

"Sir, if you are the God of the Christians you must know that I must first conquer Rome before I become the sole emperor. That may be difficult. I have fewer troops than Maxentius, and the city of Rome is protected by a mighty wall."

"Constantine, why do you doubt me? Have faith in me. I will tell you how to conquer Rome. Follow my instructions and you will be victorious."

"What would you have me do, Oh Christian God?" Constantine's face took on a keen look.

"First promise me that you will stop the persecution of Christians and allow all people to worship freely. Return church property that your predecessors have seized and compensate the Christians who have been tortured and wronged. Stop building temples to your false gods and build Christian churches instead."

"I will gladly do that."

"There is one other thing. I want all the people in your empire to accept me as the one true God."

Constantine hesitated. "Sir, you are asking a lot. The Romans love their gods and will not give them up easily. That will take time."

"Time is no object. I have eternity."

Constantine was silent, his mind preoccupied with what he heard. When he spoke it was with a firm voice. "I will do as you say. Tell me how to defeat Maxentius and you will be the God of the Roman Empire."

"Go into battle with the cross as your sign. Place it

on the shields and helmets of your soldiers and the battle standards of your army. Wear the cross on your armor and on your helmet. With the cross you will conquer."

"I will follow your instructions and lead my army to victory."

"Constantine, there's one final thing. As you rule the empire let my teachings be your guide. Demonstrate the Christian values by your actions. Be just and merciful. Love your neighbor, fill your heart with goodwill and you will enter my Kingdom."

"Where is your Kingdom?"

"My Kingdom is not of this world. It is in the heavens above. When you die you will enter it for eternity, but only if you have lived by my commandments."

"I will strive to live by your teachings."

"Constantine, you are by nature generous and caring, but you are also short tempered and quick to judge, and you have been brutal. Your anger had often led to violence and revenge. As emperor you will face many challenges both public and personal. Refrain yourself from hasty decisions. Be not vengeful. Above all do not murder, for you cannot undo a murder."

The figure faded and the light disappeared.

Constantine sat up and opened his eyes. He wiped the sweat from his face. He was trembling, not from fear but emotion. He rang for his servant and gave the order. "Awake my commanders and have them come to my tent."

When all had arrived, Constantine spoke. "Jesus

Christ, the Christian God appeared before me. He told me with his cross I will conquer. I command you to paint the cross on the shields and helmets of my soldiers and display it on the battle standards. We shall march to war under the Christian sign."

The commanders left to fulfill his orders. Constantine picked up his armor and drew a large cross on the front. He did the same to his shield and helmet. Calling his aide he said, "carve the crosses where I drew them and fill the carvings with gold so they will shine like the sun."

He walked to where the statue of Mithras stood and looked at him with sorrow in his eyes. Biting his lip and with a strained expression on his face he muttered the words. "You have given me victories and glory. You have stood by my side and guided my steps. I have loved and honored you."

He paused with labored breathing, struggling to hold back emotion. "Yet the time has come to....." Not willing to utter the words he lifted the statue and gently removed it from the pedestal.

He picked up two sticks and tied a cross. With a look of intense anticipation he said, "I am ready to fight under your sign, Oh Christian God. Bring me victory and I will build your Church and make you a mighty God of the Roman Empire."

His mind at ease he lay down to rest before the battle. He will be victorious and true to his promise, and make Christianity the religion of the Empire.

Chapter 2

Thirteen Years Later A.D. 325, Early March Imperial Palace in Nicomedia, Asia Minor

Emperor Constantine, sole ruler of the Roman Empire sat on his throne awaiting news of the Christian infighting in Alexandria, Egypt. He stomped his foot showing his impatience at the late arrival of his envoy whom he had sent to appease the Christians. Behind him a large crucifix was nailed to the wall, and a painting of the passion of Christ stood on an easel close by.

In recent months serious hostilities had arisen among the Christians in Alexandria. The conflict centered on whether Jesus Christ was equal to, or subordinate to God the Father, and had only come to earth to save humanity. Everyone had an opinion, and ordinary citizens took to the streets in demonstrations defending their position.

When the trouble first began Constantine sent a letter to the opposing factions telling them to settle their differences in peace. The message went unheeded. Conflict continued even escalated with no resolution in sight. He then sent an envoy to the opposing leaders in Alexandria whose mission was to talk to them and find a solution that would be acceptable to both sides. After waiting for weeks for his envoy to return, he was informed today that he had arrived with a full report.

Prior to his departure the envoy had briefed the emperor on the theological differences that divided the Christians. On one side of the dispute was the bishop of Alexandria, a powerful leader who believed that Jesus was God. His theology rested on the premise that Jesus Christ was equal to God the Father, the Only Begotten Son of God, born of the Father before all ages, of same substance as the Father, divine by nature, eternal, and sent to earth to save humanity from sin. The bishop not only controlled the activities and finances of the Church, its people in Alexandria and surrounding territories, but his influence reached into the secular aspects of the empire, especially judicial and legal. In addition, his close relationship with the emperor gave him further leverage. His many followers were vocal and passionate.

His opponent was a popular priest named Arius also from Alexandria. He preached that Jesus was not God, but subordinate to God the Father, not the natural son of the Father, and not of the same substance as the Father, but an adopted son sent to earth to save humanity from sin. In the minds of Arius and his followers, Jesus was only human, not divine, and not eternal, and there was a time when he did not exist. Arius also had many followers who were just as passionate.

Constantine could not understand the reasons for the dispute. After all, Christians agreed that Jesus Christ was a holy man and son of God the Father, natural or adopted, it did not matter. Whether He was God or not was not important. He wondered why such pettiness would lead to hostilities and fighting, and escalate to the point that chaos replaced order and jeopardized the security of his empire. Whether God or not made no difference to him and shouldn't to anyone else.

Waiting for his secretary's arrival Constantine's thoughts took him back in time. The path to becoming the sole emperor of the Roman Empire had not been easy. He had won the battle at the Milvian Bridge thirteen years ago, a great victory in the name of Jesus Christ. However, the circumstances at the time had forced him to share power with Licinius, his sister's husband. After twelve years of shared power, Licinius, in the eyes of Constantine, had become a threat, and all indications were that he may seize power for himself. It was then that Constantine decided to eliminate him and his young nephew, barely nine years old, so as not to leave a line to dethrone him. For a brief moment guilt overtook him as the image of his sister's inconsolable face appeared before him. He recalled the words Jesus Christ had said to him thirteen years ago. "Do not murder for it cannot be reversed." Yet he quickly dismissed the words and instead vowed to ask God again for forgiveness.

He stepped in front of a mirror and adjusted his jeweled crown which had shifted slightly. It resembled laurel leaves, a sign of victory. He was careful not dislodge the gold head band on his forehead which his servant had so carefully placed. Short hair dyed black and curled by his hairdresser was neatly arranged around his head. His long face clean shaven by his barber displayed the round chin and strong cheek bones. Large hazel eyes set close together emphasized his prominent nose. A purple robe adorned with pearls trailed behind him, and his diamond rings sparkled as he opened and closed his fists in rapid motion. He had come a long way since being a soldier.

He walked by the tall marble columns which embraced the periphery of the throne room and the bronze busts of Roman generals whose victories made Rome a great empire. Spectacular arches with exquisite carvings of Roman battles, many of them with him at the helm, linked the main room with adjacent chambers where he often held private meetings. He stopped by the central arch to look at the marble statue of himself, five times the life size, wielding a sword at the battle of the Milvian Bridge. He smiled, pride sweeping his face as he reminisced the great victory that gave him the empire.

At his feet the mosaic floor shined in brilliant colors depicting a she wolf feeding Romulus and Remus, the founders of Rome. He was fond of repeating the story of Rome's founders. They were twin baby boys, heirs to a kingdom in Italy whose uncle ordered them killed so he could be king himself. But the soldiers disobeyed the order and saved them by putting them in a cradle in the river Tiber. When the cradle floated ashore a she wolf gathered them and nursed them until a shepherd rescued them and took them in. When the boys grew up they killed their uncle and began to build a new city on the Tiber. But the boys quarreled and Romulus killed Remus and named the city of Rome after himself.

Walking past the east wall Constantine stopped to admire a magnificent fresco of his coronation as the sole ruler of the Roman Empire. It had only recently been finished, the plaster not yet dry. He saw himself seated on a throne with a halo above his head holding a cross. In the background a map of the Roman Empire stretched from Spain in the west to Syria in the east, north to Britain and south to Egypt. Yes, he was emperor, the Christian God's beloved and anointed one.

"Sire," a voice interrupted his thoughts as an elderly man wearing a bishop's attire entered the room. His grey hair lay neatly arranged on his shoulders. A Spaniard by birth and a Roman citizen, his olive complexion and large dark eyes contrasted with Constantine's fair looks. Loyal to the emperor for many years he had become his confidant and the chief advisor on Christian matters.

"Come in my good man," the emperor said seating himself on the throne and pointing to a chair on the side. He liked to receive his subjects, even bishops, sitting on the throne. It gave him a feeling of strength and power, and communicated to his visitors that he was the sole ruler on all matters, all the time.

"Your majesty," the bishop began. "I bring troubling news from Alexandria. Infighting continues between Christians. The situation is more serious than I thought."

"Are they still quarreling whether Jesus is God or not?"

"Yes, Sire, and the arguments have escalated to physical force. Street fighting has turned deadly and both sides had committed atrocities. The bishop of Alexandria expelled the priest Arius from the Church. Bishops of the empire, priests and ordinary citizens are at war defending their position with violence. There is chaos on the streets of Alexandria and may spread to other cities. People are getting hurt. Life in Alexandria has become brutal and dangerous. It is not what Christ intended."

"What is wrong with these Christians?" Constantine said in disgust. "Aren't they supposed to love each other? Don't they all believe that Jesus is the Redeemer? What does it matter whether He is God or not?"

"Sire, it matters. This is a serious theological issue which must be resolved if Christianity is to flourish. This controversy has been around for generations and now it has gotten out of hand. It is time to settle it once and for all."

"The issue is trivial," Constantine shouted slamming his fists on the armrests of his throne. "The bishops are quarreling because they have too much time on their hands. They don't have enough to do. For all I have done for the Christians, can't they at least settle their difference in peace?"

"Sire, everyone knows you have done great things for them. You have....."

"I know what I have done, you don't have to remind me," Constantine yelled. "I compensated them for their suffering during the persecutions. I returned their property that the state has seized. I gave them back their jobs and restored their civil rights. The Christian priests no longer pay taxes and have the same exemptions as the pagan priests." He stopped to catch his breath then carried on. "Who stopped building pagan temples and built Christian churches instead? Who forbade animal sacrifices? Who gave money for Christian schools? Who built homes for retired priests? I did all this and more. What else do they want these quarrelsome Christians?" He flung his hands in the air.

"The empire has many Christians now and different doctrines have emerged. Emotions run deep and tempers flare," the bishop said.

"These different doctrines divide the Church and threaten my empire. The pagans are rejoicing as the Christians fight, making themselves the laughing stock of the empire. I want Christianity to strengthen and unify my empire, not to divide it. I want peace and security, instead I have war and chaos." He groaned and covered his face with his hands.

"Sire, I have thought this through and have a solution."

"I'm listening," Constantine said with impatience.

"There has been talk among the bishops that a council is needed to standardize Church issues unrelated to this problem. I suggest you convene such a council and use it to persuade the bishops to reject the teachings of Arius. The bishops would not oppose you. After all, you have saved the Church, made the bishops the princes of the Church, and Christianity your empire's religion. They owe you."

Constantine lifted his head and smiled faintly. Yes, they owed him, irrespective of the sins he committed. He had saved Christianity and was God's beloved servant even if not yet baptized. True, he committed grave sins when seizing power and will have to sin again to stabilize the empire. He did not become the sole ruler of the Roman Empire by being nice to his adversaries. Baptism will have to wait until he finishes his work. Yes, the future may be brutal. It may be sinful. But he has to do what has to be done. When his work is finished and his death is at hand, only then will he be baptized and wash his sins away. He will be pure and enter the Kingdom of Heaven instantly.

Yet as he thought this through, he realized his sins will leave a dark shadow over him and his empire. A Church council would redeem him before God and his subjects.

"And where do you suggest I hold this council," Constantine asked.

"The city of Ankara is a possibility."

Constantine thought for a moment. "Ankara is too far inland. The old bishops, some of them lame and blind would have difficulty getting there. A better location would be my palace on the Lake of Nicaea. The air in Nicaea is healthy, the scenery magnificent, and the water in the lake is warm and soft. I think the bishops would enjoy it."

The bishop nodded in approval. "Sire, Nicaea is a perfect choice. The palace is larger than your other palaces, and would easily accommodate the bishops and their staff." The bishop knew Constantine's ulterior motive for wanting the meeting in Nicaea. It was close to his palace in Nicomedia where he could keep an eye on the council and control its proceedings.

'It's final, then," Constantine said happy that the problem was solved. He rose indicating the meeting was over. "Send out invitations to all the bishops in the empire. Inform them they will be my guests in Nicaea and I will pay their travel expenses."

Before escorting his secretary out he said, "I have high hopes this conference will end the dispute and bring harmony and peace to the Church and my empire."

"Sire, I pray it will," the bishop said trying to look confident. But as he walked to his quarters a shadow of doubt came over him. Will the bishops be willing to reach a unanimous decision on Christ's Divinity, or will they fight defending their positions? And which side will the emperor take, considering he changes his mind at random? It remained to be seen.

He reached his quarters and called to his secretary. "Send out invitations to all the bishops of the empire. Tell them the emperor is calling for a council to regulate and standardize Church practices as well as settle once and for all the question of Jesus' Divinity. The emperor will pay their travel expenses and host them in his palace at Nicaea. The conference will be held in late May."

Saying this he walked to the chapel and knelt in front of a statue of Crucified Christ. "You are God and the Only Begotten Son of the Father," he prayed. "Give safe passage to the bishops as they travel to Nicaea and fill them with faith and wisdom as they debate Christian theology and the future of the Christian Church. May your will be done."

Having finished his prayer he returned to his quarters and called for his servant to bring him supper.

Chapter 3

B ishop Caelius sat by the fire in the church rectory in the suburb of Rome, warming his feet and rubbing his hands. It had been a cold winter and spring offered no relief. He removed his eye patch that he had been wearing for twenty years, and rubbed an ointment into his empty socket, then put his eye patch back adjusting the band around his head. The patch was a part of him now, a link to the past, after a Roman soldier cut out his eye during the Christian persecutions when he refused to sacrifice to the god Jupiter.

He still could recall the horrific pain as the soldier dug a knife into his eye then beat him and sent him to the mines to do hard labor. A fellow prisoner had given him a cloth which he pressed into the socket to stop the bleeding. If he hadn't done that he probably would have bled to death. The socket still caused him pain which intensified during the cold weather. In spite of all the suffering he endured during the persecutions, he never wavered in his faith in Jesus Christ. Today, the missing eye was his mark of distinction. He was proud to have refused to worship the pagan gods. Neither did he hand to the Roman authorities the Bible and his sacred chalice as ordered, but buried them instead behind his house.

Yet there were many Christians who surrendered under torture unable to bear the pain. He did not blame them. Not everyone had the inner strength or the physical will to resist. Even though they yielded, he still considered them good Christians and argued against excluding them from serving the Church. Unfortunately not all clergy agreed, creating further friction among the Christians.

He wrapped his tunic closer to his body, put on long socks before tying his sandals, and placed his felt cap over his head. Still, he felt the chill.

"Florus, bring my toga," he called out to his servant.

An old man came carrying the long white woolen garment on his arm. He walked with a limp, his right leg muscles severed by the soldiers during the persecutions. Helping the bishop rise he began to wrap the garment around him.

"If I wasn't so cold I wouldn't bother with it. It's so difficult to put it on right but it keeps my body warm," the bishop muttered to himself struggling with the folds.

Florus added more wood to the fire and disappeared behind a curtain. Few minutes later he came back. "A courier arrived with a letter for you," he said in a loud voice handing the bishop a large envelope.

The bishop examined the seal squinting his one eye. It was the seal of his imperial majesty Emperor Constantine from his palace in Nicomedia, in the eastern part of the empire. He rubbed his eye to make sure what he saw was correct then called his niece Anastasia.

"Child, come here and read the letter to me. Something is going on in the empire and I have a nasty feeling it's not good."

Anastasia came in and kissed her uncle on the cheek. Her blue eyes conveyed tenderness and her long brown hair brushed against his face. She looked younger than her twenty two years, yet there was a seriousness about her which reflected her studious nature. She took the letter from his hands, slit open the seal and began to read.

"*From the Imperial Secretariat of Emperor Constantine to His Excellency Bishop Caelius of Italy:*"

"Louder, my child," the bishop shouted turning his good ear towards her.

She raised her voice. "*His Majesty Emperor Constantine requests your presence at a conference of bishops to be held at the emperor's palace at Nicaea in late May.*" She stopped. "I know what this is all about, uncle, it….."

"Go on my child. Finish reading the letter. We'll have plenty of time to discuss it later."

She continued. "*Several issues including the question of Jesus' Divinity are tearing the Church apart and threatening its very existence. For the sake of a unified empire and the security of the Church, the emperor has convened a council of bishops to rule on these matters and end once and for all the controversies that have plagued the Church for several decades. It is his majesty's wish that you attend the council and be his guest at the palace. Your travelling expenses as well as your staff's will be paid by the imperial treasury. Vouchers for the use of government post houses where fresh horses, lodgings, and meals will be available for you are included in the package."*

"So it has come to that," the bishop said stroking his eye patch as he felt a sudden throbbing of the socket. "It's those eastern bishops that are causing the trouble and challenging the Divinity of Jesus. Here in the west most of us are united in the Trinity and the belief that Jesus is equal to God the Father." He made the sign of the cross and whispered the words, "God the Father, God the Son, and God the Holy Spirit."

Anastasia took her uncle's hands and spoke. "There are references in the Gospel alluding to the subordinate nature of Jesus. I can quote you passages." Seeing her uncle frown she stopped. "I'm only playing the devil's advocate. There will be those who will quote the Gospel to prove their point."

"Yes child, they will indeed and we must be informed to defend our side. Start making a list of the passages that might give us trouble and construct solid arguments to justify our belief."

The bishop closed his one eye and his lips moved in silence. When he had finished his prayer he said, "I must start getting ready for the voyage. In my elderly and disabled state I need someone to accompany me besides Florus. He can take care of my physical needs but I need someone to be my eyes and ears during this conference." He looked at Anastasia.

Her eyes sparkled and her expression took on a look of exuberance. "Of course, uncle. I would have been the first to suggest it. I will get ready and send the emperor your confirmation."

Saying that she removed the eye patch from her uncle's eye, washed his eye socket with a warm brew and replaced the eye patch. Kissing him on the cheek she left the room humming to herself.

Chapter 4

Anastasia leaned over the railing and felt nauseated as she looked at the waves hitting against the ship. Her tunic and coat clung to her slim body and the wind blew in her face sweeping her hair away from her face. She loosened her veil from around her neck and felt some relief from the sickness.

It was late April and she, her uncle, and Florus were on the way to Nicaea. They had boarded a ship on the southern coast of Italy and were sailing east to Greece on the Adriatic Sea. From Greece they would travel by land to Thessalonica then to Byzantium or the New Rome which the emperor had renamed, finally taking a ferry to Nicaea. If there were no delays the journey would last several weeks and it would not be an easy one for Anastasia. She held on to her stomach as another attack of nausea overtook her. The air was hot for this time of the year and even though it was dry, the northeast wind from the mountains didn't help much.

In a strange way she already missed Rome. It was her home, where she was born and where she grew up.

The only time she had left the city was in year 313 when she was ten years old. Her uncle took her north to Milan when Emperor Constantine of the Western Empire and Emperor Licinius of the Eastern Empire proclaimed the Edict of Milan which established religious freedom for all citizens of the Roman Empire. For the first time since the terrible persecutions by Emperor Diocletian in year 303 and others before him, Christians were given the right to worship freely alongside the pagans, with no restrictions. The trip to Milan would live in her memory forever.

The ceremony had been solemn yet with much pomp and splendor. Both emperors made patriotic speeches, several bishops prayed and conducted Christian services, and church choirs sang sacred songs in the open air. Free food and drink were distributed to the people, and small wooden crosses were handed out to those who wanted them. Candidates for political offices walked around, greeting people and shaking hands. The Christians were ecstatic and celebrated with gusto. They sang and danced in the street and paid tribute to Constantine.

The pagans came to the ceremony out of curiosity and watched with interest. Some of them called the event unpatriotic, others with religious inclinations felt it betrayed Rome's state religion and the pagan gods. And there were those who not having any faith sensed the future growth of Christianity and the impact it would have on the empire, and joined in the celebrations becoming Christian in self-interest.

The Edict of Milan ordered all property which was destroyed or seized from the Christians to be returned to them, or compensations made if destroyed. Anastasia recalled how happy her uncle had been when the church in which he had officiated, where she was baptized, and which was seized by the government, was returned to him and his flock. The orphanages, the homeless shelters as well as the land which the church owned were all given back.

Her thoughts turned to her parents, especially her mother who died before she could witness Jesus' victory over the empire. She was only seven years old at the time but remembered her saintly face, never letting it fade from her memory.

Her mother came from an old aristocratic Roman family that became Christian in the 2nd century during Marcus Aurelius rule in the 160s. By the time Anastasia was born in year 303 infant baptisms in her family were common, so Anastasia was baptized in her second week of life.

Her mother had been active in the Church from her youth, becoming a deaconess at an early age, before Anastasia was born. She had survived the first wave of Christian persecution under Emperor Diocletian in 303, and had often said it was Anastasia who saved her life because the Romans were reluctant to execute pregnant women.

During a second wave of persecution in 310 she was arrested again but this time nothing could save her life.

When Emperor Licinius' soldiers came to her home and ordered her to worship Jupiter, she refused. Her congregation wanted to save her and volunteered to bribe the Roman soldiers to let her go free. Others offered to sacrifice to Jupiter in her place which the Romans would have allowed. Still others asked her to go through the motions and pretend to worship Jupiter. And there were those who were willing to die in her place. All to no avail. She went to her death holding a cross and singing a hymn, begging God to take care of her child. At her beheading heavy rain fell, but at the moment when the executioner raised the ax, the sun came out and a rainbow appeared in the sky. Even the soldiers were taken aback and bowed their heads.

Losing her mother was especially hard on Anastasia because she lost her father only a few months before. He was a Roman officer often away on military campaigns. Of German decent he was not a Christian but sympathetic to the new religion and did not object to his wife's faith. In year 310 during a battle in Spain he was killed. She did not remember him and saw him only a few times in her life, the last time when he came home on a furlough.

He stayed for a month and when it was time for him to leave he lifted his little daughter, kissed her, then placed her on his knee and put her little hands in his. "If I rub my hands against your soft skin my callouses will go away," he had said. She remembered checking his hands to see if the callouses had disappeared, but they were still there. When he left she never saw him again.

Her mother cried for days when news of his death arrived. They had been much in love, sweethearts from an early age. "He had only a few more years to retirement and lived for the day when he could be with his family," her mother murmured between her wails.

The army honored him according to pagan rites, but when her mother claimed his body she gave him a secret Christian burial. As a Roman soldier who died in the line of duty her mother received a widow's pension which secured Anastasia's education.

Whether it was her father's death or the escalation of Christian persecution, or both, her mother changed. She no longer had the will to live. She stayed in her room and seldom came out. The only activities that gave her meaning were her duties as a deaconess. And so, soon after her father's funeral her mother went willingly to her own death.

Anastasia remembered her mother's last words. "If I am to die your uncle my brother will take care of you. He is a good man, a bishop of the Church. He will love you as his own and give you a good education. I will watch over you from above, my little angel."

Her words came true. Her uncle doted on her. Having been widowed himself and having no living children he took her in as his own daughter. When the persecutions ended and the Church surfaced from under the ground, she became a pupil at a formal Christian school for girls, no longer having to attend in secret. As she grew older, she became immersed in her studies of the Gospel and the life of Jesus and the apostles, and never lost her desire to serve the Church. Her mother's work as deaconess and leader in her congregation inspired her to follow in her footsteps. She had big dreams for herself, many of them in the service of the Church, and with the evolving changes she hoped she might serve Christ on an even higher level than a deaconess.

"Here you are child," she heard her uncle's voice which brought her back to reality. "I've been looking for you. We will soon reach the coastline."

She looked to the distance and saw the oblong islands, some large and some small adorning the Greek coast. How beautiful and peaceful she thought.

As they approached the coast, the busy port came into view with sailors loading and unloading cargo, ships pulling in and out of port, and merchants selling their wares. Anastasia felt a sense of excitement having lived in the suburbs of Rome and not encountering the cosmopolitan flavor of a busy port.

The ship reached the harbor and Anastasia and the bishop disembarked. Florus turned his attention to bringing the luggage on land, and Anastasia looked at her surroundings.

People moving in all directions and speaking foreign languages dominated the landscape. Anastasia recognized Greek but the other languages were foreign to her.

Slaves with branded foreheads, dressed in rags, some

of them with heads half shaved and welts on bodies from beatings, carried bags of textiles and jugs of honey and wine from Syria, ready to sail to Rome. Others carrying stones of marble on their bent backs from the quarries in Greece, made their way in single file towards the waiting ships. Sweat mingled with blood run down their bodies and mosquitoes buzzed around them. Anastasia tried to turn away but her eyes were fixed on the misery before her. She asked herself again as she often did, why did slavery exist? Why didn't the bishops condemn it? Why didn't Christianity denounce it?

She tried to remember if the Gospels condemned slavery. She didn't think so. In fact they seem to support it. St. Paul approved of it in his Letter to the Ephesians Chapter 6, Verse 5. *"Slaves be obedient to human masters with fear and trembling, in sincerity of heart, as to Christ, not only when being watched, as currying favor, but as slaves of Christ, doing the will of God from the heart, willingly serving the Lord and not human beings, knowing that each will be requited from the Lord for whatever good he does, whether he is slave or free."*

And why would St. Peter say in his First Letter to Christian Communities, Chapter 2, Verse 18. *"Slaves, be subject to your masters with all reverence, not only to those that are good and equitable, but also to those who are perverse. For whenever anyone bears the pain of unjust suffering because of consciousness of God, that is grace. But what credit is there if you are patient when beaten for doing wrong? But if you are patient when you suffer for doing what is good, that is a grace before God. For this you have been called, because Christ also suffered for you, leaving you an example that you should follow in his footsteps.*" Even if Peter did explain that to suffer unjustly is God's grace, why should some be slaves and suffer and others be free? Where was justice?

She turned her eyes to a group of merchants taking inventory of sacks of grain from Egypt for distribution to the poor. The emperors have given free grain to the poor from the beginning of the empire. They feared the people would revolt if hungry, but a good deed was a good deed no matter what the reason, Anastasia believed. Further down silk from China was being loaded on ships to Rome to be made into robes for the wealthy Roman ladies. She had often seen and admired the rich matrons as they travelled in their litters carried by slaves to social events.

"Come child," Bishop Caelius said taking her arm. "We must find our escort whom the emperor had sent to meet us." He was about to take a step forward when a high ranking Roman officer in full armor and a plumed helmet approached him.

"Bishop Caelius," the officer said saluting him. "My name is Valerius and I am in the service of Emperor Constantine. I am here to escort you and your staff safely to Nicaea." He glanced at Anastasia and a slight look of surprise came over his face.

"Thank you. My niece Anastasia and my servant Florus are travelling with me," the bishop said turning to Anastasia who was standing by him and to Florus who was guarding the luggage.

Valerius smiled at Anastasia and his face showed genuine pleasure. Pointing to a contingent of mounted soldiers and a four wheel coach hitched up to six horses he said, "come, we have only a few hours before sunset at which time we shall stop at a post house for the night."

Having spoken he lead the way. Anastasia took her uncle's arm and Florus took the other and the three walked towards the carriage.

Valerius helped the bishop into the coach, then gave his arm to Anastasia.

For a brief moment their eyes met and Anastasia saw a man with grey penetrating eyes, the kind of eyes that want to control. His skin was tanned and she attributed that to his outdoor activities.

"Thank you Officer Valerius," the bishop said situating himself in the carriage which was large enough for the three of them to sleep in.

Anastasia sat opposite her uncle and Florus made himself comfortable in the seat behind the bishop.

After the slaves had loaded the luggage the trumpeter sounded the trumpet and the carriage moved slowly out of the harbor and inland toward Thessalonica.

Anastasia crossed herself and prayed for a safe journey, a habit she always followed even when leaving the house. She felt secure knowing that most of the Christian infighting regarding Jesus' Divinity took place in Alexandria. She looked out of the carriage window and let the peaceful beauty of the mountains and the pine forests relax her.

By now her uncle and Florus had fallen asleep. The sun was beginning to set and dark clouds appeared in the sky but still there was no sign of the post house. She wondered what caused the delay but did not think it significant, and curling up on the soft seat closed her eyes.

She did not know how long she slept, perhaps few minutes, or an hour, but the sky was black when she awoke, and no moon lit the way. Only the soldiers' torches provided light. Suddenly a loud voice broke the silence.

"Keep close to the carriage and charge on my order," Valerius shouted.

Anastasia lifted the curtain from the carriage window and opened the hatch. "Are we in danger?" she called to Valerius who was riding alongside.

"No my lady, only precaution. A scout brought news that a small disturbance has taken place half way to Thessalonica. Roman troops stationed nearby have put it down, but we were forced to take a detour. Nothing to worry about, my lady. We should be at a post house shortly." With that he saluted her and galloped away.

She reclined in her seat somewhat satisfied. And yet uneasiness lingered in her mind. Was the disturbance against the Christians? Were they in danger?

She closed her eyes trying to stay calm, and in spite of her misgivings fell asleep.

Chapter 5

A sudden jolt awakened her as the carriage stopped in front of a gate where sentries with heavy armor demanded to see their passes. After obtaining clearance they entered a large courtyard where several buildings stood surrounded by a tall wall. Towers erected at top of the wall provided shelter for the lookouts. The carriage pulled up to a stone structure in the middle of the courtyard which served as the administrative building, where travelers registered and were assigned bed and meal tickets. An attendant stepped up to the carriage and helped the party disembark. Anastasia glanced around her.

In the far left corner of the clearing next to another guarded gate were the stables, and next to the stables were barracks and canteen for soldiers. To the right of the administrative building stood a two story structure where travelers slept, dined and entertained themselves. Connected to the building by a stone passage was the kitchen where cooks prepared meals for soldiers and travelers. Behind the building were the granary, a large vegetable garden, and a deep cellar where wine, meats, and produce were stored.

"My lady, I have completed the required registration and will escort your party to your quarters," Valerius said pointing the way.

Something about his voice caught Anastasia's attention. The tone was different from before. It was personal. She wasn't sure if she liked it.

She curtsied and thanked him, then took her uncle's arm and in step with Valerius and Florus walked across the courtyard to the travelers' quarters. From the corner of her eye she saw a contingent of soldiers arriving, among them two wounded ones carried on stretches.

"I will leave you now and call on you in the morning. We will depart at sunrise," Valerius said opening the door to their room. He saluted, gave her a long penetrating look, then started to leave.

"Sir, why were these soldiers wounded?" Anastasia asked.

"There's been some fighting but nothing serious," Valerius said.

"Who was fighting?" she asked with concern.

She saw him hesitate and added, "you must let me know. I handle danger better if I know the facts."

"The Christians were fighting amongst themselves. Those who believe that Jesus is God were fighting against the followers of Arius who do not believe Jesus is God. Roman guards intervened and a few were hurt. They will survive, just minor wounds. As the Christians fight amongst themselves the pagans rejoice."

"I thought they only fought in Alexandria," Anastasia said.

"No my lady. The fighting has spread to Greece." He stretched out his arm towards her as if wanting to shield her. She didn't want him to touch her and stepped back. He showed surprise, his eyes turned cool, then walked away.

She wondered about his answer but let it go and turned her attention to her surroundings. The room assigned them was plush and used for important dignitaries. It was paneled with tapestries, the beds had high canopies and drapes to keep the draft away, and a large mirror with a gold frame hung on one wall.

A servant brought their supper on a silver tray and waited on them. After eating an appetizer of sea urchins and eggs, followed by baked lamb, cooked asparagus and sweet rice, they finished off with fruits and pastries, all served with wine flavored with spices and sweetened with honey. Anastasia did not remember when she had eaten such a meal, if at all. By the time the pastries were served, the bishop had fallen asleep. A slave brought in fresh linen and nightclothes, and offered to wash the bishop, but Florus wouldn't hear of it. He put the elderly bishop to bed himself and lay down by his side on a cot. Anastasia prepared for the night and although worried about the fighting fell asleep.

"Uncle, it's time to rise and get ready for the journey," Anastasia said bending over the bishop with Florus behind her, ready to help him dress. She had been up before sunrise and although she slept well in the canopied bed, the worry and fear with which she fell asleep was with her when she awoke.

After finishing breakfast, they packed their belongings and walked to the courtyard where Valerius was waiting. He tried to be cheerful but a shadow covered his face. "We had more trouble. The Christian infighting has escalated and several priests were beaten on both sides of the dispute. I've engaged heavy guard to accompany us. Once we reach Thessalonica we will travel by sea to New Rome. You will not be able to see the beautiful Greek landscape, but you will be safe."

She turned to her uncle. "I'm afraid for you. The upcoming council of bishops has provoked more violence. They may want to kill you for believing that Jesus is God."

"Anastasia, I have lived a long life and was privileged to take part in events that changed our world and brought hope and salvation to the people. If I die today let it be God's will. But I hope God will let me witness the resolution of this controversy," the bishop said somewhat nostalgically.

They boarded the coach under guard and continued on their journey. The terrain was rugged but beautiful and Anastasia settled down for a peaceful ride. The swaying coach made her sleepy and in spite of a good night's rest she fell asleep.

Suddenly the carriage stopped. A group of men on horseback blocked their path. One of the men, young and sitting tall on his horse approached the carriage followed by five companions. None of them had weapons. "We've come to see the bishop. We heard he is on the way to Nicaea and want to have a word with him," the young man said.

"Who are you?" Valerius asked riding up to the young man.

"We are members of a local peace group both Christians and pagans that seek to prevent violence. We came in friendship and wish no harm. A group of Christians in prayer were attacked by a mob last night and some were hurt. We heard the bishop was travelling and wish to inform him."

"We know what happened. The Christians were fighting amongst themselves," Valerius snapped.

"This was not a fight between the Christians. We have evidence the attackers were Roman soldiers, perhaps a rogue group," the young man said.

"What evidence to you have?" Valerius asked, his eyes glaring at the man.

The young man opened his mouth to speak but changed his mind. "I would rather speak with civil authorities," he said with caution.

He had barely finished speaking when Valerius swung his sword and motioning to his soldiers surrounded the young man and his companions. "What do you mean rogue soldiers? Are you accusing the Roman army of subversion? "

"Nothing of the kind," the young man said his face showing fear. "It's just that some witnesses said they saw soldiers in Roman uniforms beating on the Christians. They may have been imposters. Probably they were. All we want to do is to alert the bishop and tell him to be careful." He turned to his companions and murmured something to them. They started to retreat but Valerius and his soldiers blocked them, their swords raised.

"Let us go. We are unarmed," the young man cried as he tried to back away from the soldiers.

Before he could move Valerius swung his sword at the man and without any warning plunged it into his chest. The man gave out a groan and fell to the ground in a pool of blood. His companions in shock and panic on their faces, tried to retreat, but the soldiers obeying Valerius' order began the massacre. The men fought back with whips and fists but when everything was over, the young man and his five companions lay dead on the ground. It happened fast. One minute there were six unarmed men on a peace mission, next minute they were all dead.

Anastasia had awakened and opened the carriage door. Behind her stood the bishop. Seeing the carnage horror overtook her. "What happened? Who are these men and why are they dead?" she cried, beside herself with shock.

"My lady, these men were members of a secret pagan

society that wants to do away with all Christians, whether Arians or not. They were closing in on the carriage and would have killed the bishop, and probably you and your servant. I did what I had to do."

As she looked at the dead bodies, young men, few still boys, their faces terrified, anger surged within her. "Did they have weapons?" she blurted out seeing none.

"These people know how to kill without weapons. One stroke on your neck and you are dead. They are willing to die for their cause. They terrorize the country in the name of paganism."

At that moment the bishop stepped down from the carriage. He was enraged and trembling, unsteady on his feet. "How do you know they posed danger? Did they threaten us?"

"I did what I had to do to keep you safe," Valerius said.

"Their deaths could have been averted had you let them speak to me. May God have mercy on their souls and yours for what you have done." The bishop lifted his eyes to heaven and prayed.

Valerius rode away and called to his soldiers. "Clear the bodies and bury them. We must be on our way."

The soldiers threw the six men into a ditch and flung dirt over them.

Still visibly shaken the bishop walked to the mass grave on which Florus had carved six crosses and recited the funeral rites. When he had finished the three climbed back into the carriage and the journey continued.

Nothing more was said about this but the deaths of the men lay heavy on Anastasia's mind. No one will ever know what the group's purpose was, she thought. Her opinion of Valerius deteriorated and her suspicion of him escalated. Her dislike of him increased. There was something unsettling about him and she hoped for a quick end to the journey. She did not believe the men were killers. Valerius murdered them, but why?

And so they continued east, her mind uneasy and her body shaken. They reached Thessalonica without incidents for which Anastasia was grateful. As they approached the city, she watched the beautiful harbor come into view, and the imperial palace where the emperor often stayed. Her spirits rose and she felt invigorated.

The city's history went back to three centuries before the birth of Jesus, when King Cassander of Macedonia built it and named it after his wife Thessalonica. He must have loved her very much to name a city after her, Anastasia thought. Or perhaps it was his wedding gift to her, or maybe he felt guilty because according to a legend he had captured her in a battle then made her his wife. For whatever reasons he honored her, and his actions towards her were generous and noble.

But the greatest pleasure that Anastasia derived was tracing the footsteps of St. Paul who as a missionary founded a church in Thessalonica not long after Jesus' death. During his short stay he converted many gentiles, and when he left he kept in touch with then through the letters he wrote. She had read Paul's letters to the Thessalonians and took to heart his message to lead peaceful and moral lives, to be patient, support the weak, and not return evil for evil. But when he preached that those who were unwilling to work should not eat, nor burden or depend on anyone but pay one's own keep, she had reservations. There were times when work was not available even if wanted, and not everyone was able to work. After all, would any Christian wish to have another die of starvation?

When St. Paul urged others to mind their own business, he probably meant private affairs, she thought. Because would anyone want to remain silent in sight of injustice? After all, silence was complicity. She struggled with these concepts and others like it, yet realized that three centuries ago, the outlook on life was different, and St. Paul's belief that the 2nd coming of Christ would happen soon, may have influenced his teachings. In spite of her struggles, knowing that Christ picked him for his ministry even though St. Paul himself had said he was a blasphemer, persecutor, and arrogant, strengthened her belief that he was a great apostle without whom Christianity would not have survived. As Christ showed mercy to St. Paul, so He will show mercy to all.

The carriage passed by the public bath house and Anastasia thoughts turned to Rome. Every morning when it was the time for women to bathe, she paid her entrance fee, which was higher for women than men, and which she resented but nevertheless paid, and began her bath.

There was a ritual which she and the Romans followed. First came working out in the exercise yard. Her favorite was rolling a metal hoop around the area or throwing a ball with her friends. She then spread oil on her body and scraped off the dirt before jumping into a very hot pool to wash off the dirt. She had to wear sandals because the floor was too hot for bare feet. The pools were heated by furnaces in the basement which sent warm air to the floors and walls of the pools.

Once her body was cleaned came the part she liked best, a dip in a lukewarm pool where she relaxed and cooled off. Finally she jumped into a cold outside pool where she practiced her swimming and often raced with her friends. The baths kept her healthy and clean, and gave her an occasion to meet friends and catch up on the news.

Yet her pleasure was mixed with guilt at the misery of the slaves who maintained the furnaces, and whose constant contact with the heat left them weak and prone to fainting, even death. Now as the carriage drove by the baths she pictured the slaves throwing wood into the furnaces, their faces blistered from the flames, their arms burned, their breathing labored from the smoke. How many of them would faint or even die today? The feeling of revulsion came over her, and again she questioned slavery and the reasons for its existence.

Continuing through the streets of Thessalonica she watched vendors selling hot pies, stews, and sausages. Further down fresh fruit lay neatly displayed in a kiosk, and jars of sweet wine stood ready for thirsty customers. As in Rome, most people bought their meals from food bars outside, eliminating the risk of fire from cooking at home. Some neighborhoods forbade to cook at home because the wooden apartments were prone to fire.

They approached the imperial palace and the sight of it was dazzling. The first thing that caught the eye was the magnificent garden surrounding the palace proper. Red, yellow, and white flowers bloomed in single rows culminating in diametrical designs bordering a colonnaded courtyard. Apricot and peach trees planted between the columns further graced the courtyard, sweetening the air and providing a cool breeze. In the middle of the courtyard stood a decorative fountain with a round basin made of pink marble with descending steps to the stream. In the middle of the basin was a gold pedestal carved with the head of a she wolf from whose mouth a stream of water flowed colored with a white dye resembling milk. Within the courtyard stood statues of Roman generals, the largest of Constantine himself.

"We will rest at the palace for a few days before sailing to Constantinople," Valerius said brining his horse to the carriage and leaning inside. He hesitated then added, "perhaps when you have rested, you and the bishop will do the honor of sharing a meal with the host and hostess residing at the palace."

They accepted the invitation with reluctance. Neither the bishop nor Anastasia wanted to go but etiquette demanded that they accept.

Chapter 6

After settling in the palace guest rooms and resting, a slave came to escort the bishop and Anastasia to the banquet hall in the imperial palace, where tables and couches stood ready for the evening meal. At the entrance another slave removed their sandals and washed their feet. An usher announced their arrival and as their names were being called, Anastasia saw Valerius walking towards them.

"Welcome," he said bowing, then looked straight at Anastasia with intensity. She returned his look but only for a moment. She felt uneasy. He no longer had his uniform, instead he wore a short white tunic and a red cloak over his shoulders fastened by a gold pin. His brown hair visible for the first time without his helmet was cropped neatly around his head. His clean shaven face was smooth and tanned.

He escorted them in the direction of the raised platform where guests of honor sat. At that point Anastasia entered a world which she had not known before. Glittering chandeliers hung from the ceiling. Beautiful mosaics of Greek mythology decorated the floors. Artemis, the goddess of hunt, virility and childbirth, and protector of girls stood in a forest clearing surrounded by trees. Her hair loose on her shoulders, her face lit by the moonlight, she held a bow and arrow ready to aim. Next to her Poseidon, the god of sea and the protector of waters, stood tall clutching a long spear with three prongs. And Penelope, the faithful wife weaving a shroud during the day and unraveling it each night to keep her suitors at bay until her husband Odysseus returned, adorned the center of the floor. The walls of the hall were painted with frescoes depicting gods and goddesses of pagan Rome. On one wall was Venus, the goddess of love, as she emerged from sea on a shell surrounded by doves and sparrows. Facing the entrance was Minerva, the goddess of wisdom springing fully armed with helm, spear, and shield from the head of Jupiter, the supreme god. Across Jupiter was Flora the goddess of spring strolling lightly through the fields picking flowers.

As she walked towards the raised platform, Anastasia gazed at the ladies in colored silk robes and jeweled rings on every finger, reclining on the couches alongside long tables where food was being served. Gold and silver necklaces adorned their necks and dangling earrings chimed as they moved their heads from side to side conversing with guests. Their pale faces and bare arms whitened with chalk gave them a statuesque appearance. Lips painted with red dye and eyebrows darkened with ash, accentuated their paleness and added to their beauty, making them look like goddesses. Men in long robes and laurel leaves in their hair reclined beside the ladies in jovial party spirits.

Valerius guided them to a cushioned couch on the platform at which a man of middle age stood awaiting them. Next to him, reclining on a couch was a woman with the most elegant coiffure Anastasia had ever seen. Curled locks arranged in a tall pile adorned the front of her head, while in the back several braids arranged in decreasing circles created a ripple effect.

As they neared the couch the man approached them, bowed and extended his arm. "I am Paulus, your host, the emperor's representative in Thessalonica. This is my wife Sabina," he said gesturing to the woman on the couch.

The woman rose and smiled. She was a beauty, a head taller than her husband. "This banquet is in your honor," she said softly. As she turned around motioning them to sit, Anastasia saw that her high hairdo made her look taller from the front than the back. When they were seated she called to a slave who washed their hands with perfumed water.

Wealthy Romans reclined when they ate so Valerius motioned to Anastasia to do the same and placed himself next to her.

The slaves began to bring arrays of exquisite dishes prepared in an artistic fashion and decorated with flowers. They placed them on long tables alongside the reclining guests who reached out to the dishes with their fingers. In between courses slaves washed the guests' hands. The first course Anastasia tasted was a dish of hard boiled eggs with mushrooms and sardines cooked with mild pepper plant. It was delicious and served with a spicy sauce if the guests requested. Ham in sweet sauce and pickled fish, then nuts, fruits and honey cakes followed. Slaves poured sweet wine flavored with honey and spices into silver goblets.

Valerius bent towards Anastasia and touched her arm. "My lady, your presence inspires me. I hope once we reach Nicaea, we may see each other often."

Anastasia faked a smile and pulled away. Unsure what to say, she remained silent.

"Tell me more about yourself," he said.

"I live with my uncle, the bishop, and spend my time serving the Church," she said reluctantly hoping he would not ask any more questions.

"What do you want out of life?" Valerius continued.

How impertinent of him to ask this, she thought, nevertheless she answered. "In time I hope to become a deaconess, maybe even a priest and serve God."

"Beauty like yours would be wasted if it didn't belong to a man."

How dare he to speak to her as if she could be owned, she thought. Keeping her resentment to herself, she said, "Sir, I am my own person and will not belong to anyone." She wanted to say more but prudence kept her silent. In due time she will speak if necessary.

The sound of music broke the awkward silence. Two male slaves dressed as musicians in short black tunics, one with a flute and another with a lyre were playing a love song. A beautiful slave girl in a white silk robe and a garland of lilies in her long black hair, walked to the reclining guests and sang of love, her voice soft and passionate. When she came to Anastasia she sang of two lovers binding their hearts forever and vanishing into the clouds on silver wings. Valerius leaned over to Anastasia and kissed her hand. She pulled away.

"I'm sorry my lady if I offend you," he said sensing her displeasure. "From the moment I saw you I was drawn to you. Please don't think this is trivial. I have never felt like this before."

She remained silent, confused and annoyed.

The banquet continued with entertainment and mingling of guests. It was time for the games and Valerius turned to Anastasia. "My lady, the host will now engage the guests in a game. His favorite game is the numbers game. He will pick a number, for example, five, and the guests will be required to do whatever he tells them five times. The rumor is that he will pick number three and will ask his guests to kiss their neighbors three times. For some it could be a kiss on the cheek, but in our case I hope it's more than that."

Anastasia knew it was time to go. She could never kiss Valerius. She found him repulsive. She turned to the bishop who by now was sleeping and nudged him. "Uncle it is time to go. We've had a long day and need our rest."

"But my lady, the games are just beginning. Will you

not stay?" Valerius said trying to hide his anger, yet his eyes revealed his feelings.

Anastasia ignored him. Afraid of what she might say, she did not reply. Helping her uncle rise, she took him by the arm and walked away.

Valerius was silent, and with a stern face escorted them to the door then went back to the party.

They reached their rooms and settled for the night. As Anastasia lay in bed she recalled Valerius' eyes and they frightened her.

Chapter 7

Anastasia and her uncle spent two days in Thessalonica enjoying the sights and the hospitality of their hosts. They visited the magnificent Arch of Galerius which Galerius built in 298 in honor of his victory against the Persians, as well as the spectacular Rotunda which he built as a mausoleum for himself, although he was not buried there. Constantine converted it into a Christian church and Anastasia stopped at the church to pray. In the middle of the city was the Forum, alive with merchants and shoppers from all over the empire, whose strange languages and attire captured her interest.

As a parting gift from the hosts Anastasia received a gold broach designed in the shape of a dolphin, and the bishop a new white toga which he badly needed. After taking in the baths and saying farewell to their hosts and guests, the party boarded a ship at the beautiful harbor and set sail to Constantinople on their way to Nicaea.

Anastasia was grateful that during this part of the trip Valerius did not pester her, yet she couldn't shed her anxiety. At times he was cheerful but aloof and other times he sulked like a child who didn't get his way. Was he enough of a man to accept rejection, she asked herself, or did he have a dark side that would complicate her life, maybe even endanger it?

They reached the beautiful shores of New Rome, named so by Emperor Constantine, but known for centuries as Byzantium. It was an ancient Greek city going back centuries before Jesus' birth. Constantine was rebuilding it as a Christian city and already people were calling it Constantinople, the city of Constantine.

After landing ashore a carriage took them to the central square surrounded by new public buildings. They were built and adorned with marble and tiles which Constantine had pillaged from temples in other parts of the empire. Even the tall columns that supported many of the buildings were taken from Greek shrines and transported to his New Rome. Greek and Roman statues also stolen from around the empire stood in strategic places for all to admire. To many Greeks and Romans, Constantine's robbing their cities of art to adorn his New Rome was offensive, but there was nothing they could do about it.

As the carriage advanced to the Great Palace which Constantine had built for himself, Anastasia caught a glimpse of the Hippodrome where the chariot races were held, and further down she spotted the all-important baths.

Arriving at the palace they received a gracious welcome from the emperor's representative who assigned them magnificent rooms for the night. A banquet in their honor was planned for that evening. Valerius excused himself from the banquet citing business to which he had to attend. Anastasia breathed a sigh of relief. She would enjoy the celebration without the anxiety of having him close.

When it was time for the banquet, a beautiful slave girl escorted her and the bishop to the hall where over a hundred guests awaited them. When the usher announced their names, the guests including senators, merchants, artists and their wives rose in unison as the musicians played the trumpets. Anastasia and the bishop were seated on a platform from which they admired the glamor of the hall, and listened to a play performed in their honor. It had a Christian theme and had not been staged before.

It was a story of a young pagan girl who was orphaned when her parents were killed in a fire. Not having a place to go, she wandered from place to place until she stumbled upon a Christian settlement where she received food and shelter, and where the Christian people nurtured her. With their love she grew up to be kind and caring. Grateful for the help she received she became a Christian and stayed with the community. Then one day a delegation arrived from a foreign country and informed her that she was the lost princess they were looking for, and the only surviving member of the royal family. Her people wanted her to be crowned queen. She accepted their offer and when she became the queen she converted her kingdom to Christianity. It was an inspiring story played by talented actors who blended music, poetry and dancing.

The banquet was coming to a close and Anastasia was ready to retire when suddenly the stomping of feet and loud voices interrupted the festivity. A group of about twenty men waving sticks and dressed in tunics with the letter A sewn on the front, were trying to gain entrance to the hall. The guards at the entrance were furiously trying to keep them away. Within minutes another group of men appeared, also waving sticks, and began to attack the first group. They wore tunics with letters GS sewn in the front. They also numbered about twenty.

Overtaking the guards the fight entered the banquet hall. The guests realizing that danger was looming began to scream, some hid under the tables, and others cowered anticipating blows. Anastasia swung her arm around her uncle and guiding him to a column hid behind it.

The host afraid for the safety of his guests stood upon a table and yelled. "Everyone move to the hallway. Hurry."

Anastasia grabbed the bishop's arm and pulled him into the long hallway connecting the banquet hall to the kitchens. Someone bolted the heavy door to the hall. From the kitchens the smells of cooking food lingered in the air.

"What is happening?" Anastasia shouted to a guard.

"The Christians are fighting the Christians. It's a backlash against the Council to be held in Nicaea. The ones with the A on their tunics are the Arians who barged in to create havoc. Those with GS signify God the Son, and have tried to dispel them." Seeing Anastasia's frightened face he said, "you will be safe. A backup of soldiers is on the way."

For the next hour the guests sat in fear as the scuffle continued. They held on to one another and whispered amongst themselves. Most prayed to Jesus, few to their pagan gods. The host moved among the guests trying to reassure them. When he came to the bishop he said, "it's strange the Christians are fighting here. It doesn't follow logic. This is a Christian city and most of the Christians believe in the Trinity. We have not had disturbances before."

The bishop thought for a minute then said, "this may be a sign of more trouble to come. Perhaps the division among Christians is more pronounced than we thought. Perhaps it has reached Constantinople. Only time will tell."

Yet he questioned his own statement. The fight at the banquet was out of place. Why would the Arians bring the conflict to the banquet? The fights in Alexandria took place on the streets, visible to the crowds for utmost effect. And why was the opposition so conveniently available? Above all, why did the groups identify themselves by the letters A and GS on their tunics? They did not do this in Alexandria. His thoughts were cut short when he heard frightened voices around him. Gathering his toga he walked among the guests comforting them and praying.

As soon as reinforcements arrived peace was restored and guests returned to the banquet hall. Some remained for more festivities but most retired to their homes.

Miraculously nobody was killed and only few of the men were injured. The host apologized for the disruption and ordered the guards to arrest the leaders but let the others go free.

On the way to their rooms Anastasia said to the bishop. "I'm mystified. Why were the Christians fighting in Constantinople? It's in Alexandria where the hostilities are."

"I have a nasty feeling there is something sinister about this," the bishop replied. "Honest fighting between Christians, if you can call it that, is unorganized and takes place on the streets, among passionate believers on both sides. But this fight looks like it was performed. The whole thing is out of character."

"Then why did they fight?" Anastasia asked.

"These may be attempts to weaken the emperor and the Christian Church. A stable empire depends on a strong Church, united in its theology. When Christians fight among themselves it shows the pagans how divided we are. Many pagans would like to eradicate Christianity and infighting gives them an upper hand. It leaves the emperor and the Church vulnerable. I pray this is not a conspiracy to overthrow the emperor and turn back the clock on Christianity." Seeing Anastasia's worried face, he added "my imagination is taking over. Do not fear. Trust in God."

In spite of her uncle's soothing words Anastasia's worries persisted but she kept them to herself. She went to bed glad to leave Constantinople and anxious to start the journey to Nicaea.

Chapter 8

Constantine's Palace at Nicaea

I t was a short sail from Constantinople to Nicaea, and the next day Anastasia, the bishop and Florus boarded the ferry for their final destination. With a good night's sleep, her anxiety diminished. Her heart was light and her hopes high. She was ready to put the events of the past day behind her and prepare for the Council. She had not seen Valerius and began to hope he had accepted her rejections, and would not harass her any more.

If she thought that Thessalonica and Constantinople welcomed them with pomp and ceremony, the splendor that awaited them in Nicaea surpassed everything she had seen so far. Upon their arrival Constantine's personal guards welcomed them with trumpets and fanfare, and an escort of the emperor's private entourage led them to their quarters. Having been assigned a suite of luxurious rooms, with flowing water for bathing and a terrace with view on the lake, slaves appeared to give them bath and a massage.

Both the bishop and Anastasia declined, with Florus helping the bishop, and Anastasia taking care of herself.

After having rested and feeling refreshed, they were led to a large reception hall. Upon entering Anastasia's eyes filled with amazement. She had never seen a more beautiful room and so many bishops together. She estimated there were close to three hundred bishops, dressed in long red robes and tall white miters on their heads. They were conversing in groups of various sizes, their expressions revealing the awe of the surroundings around them.

The reception hall was long and extended the length of the main palace. Arranged in strategic places were hundreds of chairs and couches upholstered in silk, and decorated with designs of colorful flowers. Against the walls stood marble tables with meats, fruits, cakes and goblets of wine. Lamps burning with olive oil gave off a sweet aroma, and crystal chandeliers with hundreds of candles brightened the hall.

The tapestries on the walls displayed Christian motifs, the largest among them the Annunciation. It depicted Mary kneeling, and the Angel Gabriel standing in front of her telling her that she will be the Mother of God. The mosaic floor gave the impression of moving water as the colors changed from blue to green giving it a rippling effect. From the ceiling a painted figure of Christ watched those below. To the right of Christ and just below was a painting of Constantine with a halo over his head, holding a cross. Behind him the words "With the cross you will conquer." Within this splendor slaves moved silently among the bishops serving refreshments and assisting those in need.

Anastasia herself in awe took a few minutes to grasp the grandeur of the scene, then turned her attention to the bishops. "Uncle, do you know these bishops?" she asked stunned by so many holy men.

"Child, I know few of them quite well, the rest I met briefly or not at all. Most are from the Eastern Empire. Only a few of us are here from the Western Empire. I see the bishops from Spain, Carthage, and Gaul, and two priests representing Pope Sylvester in Rome who is too old and sick to travel. Many from the West were unable to come for different reasons. It's a long journey for old men to undertake. Some did not want to leave their dioceses. They didn't think this meeting was important. What unites us in the West is the belief in the Trinity, that Jesus is equal to the Father. It is the eastern bishops that cause the controversy." He looked around him and said, "the eastern and western bishops seem to stay apart. I don't see them mingling."

"So many of the bishops are crippled or blind" she said looking at the mass of aged men.

"Yes, my dear. They have suffered as Christians. Many of them have been tortured in prisons, others were in the mines, and still others on the run. Most have some sort of debility. I was fortunate to lose only one eye. Others were not." He touched his eye patch as if to remind himself of his infirmity.

They moved around the hall, Bishop Caelius greeting those he knew and acquainting himself with others. Anastasia stayed by his side helping him find his way, and repeating to him their greetings when her uncle had trouble hearing.

Suddenly a trumpet sounded and a lady dressed in imperial clothing walked into the hall. She was tall and slender with an oval face, small mouth and a long straight nose. Her long red robe was adorned with diamonds, over which she wore a white shawl with sewn rubies creating a design of flowers. Her long necklace was set with pearls and emeralds, and her fingers glittered with rings of every shape and stone. On her left arm she wore a gold bracelet shaped like a dolphin with matching dangling earrings. As she made her way to the center of the hall, she moved her hands in graceful gestures, her red nails accentuating her long slim fingers. Behind her walked a young man who although had a well fitted tunic and sandals made of leather, was a slave recognized by a mark on his arm. He held a tablet and a bone stylus.

The bishops stopped chatting, and all eyes turned on the lady as she walked to a platform on which stood a couch upholstered with crimson velvet. A canopy hung over the couch which hid her face slightly. The slave followed and took his place behind her.

A courtier stepped forward and made an announcement. "May I present Her Highness, Constantia, the emperor's sister."

She nodded her head gracefully and spoke a few words

to her slave then addressed the audience. "Christian bishops of the Roman Empire. In the name of the emperor I welcome you to this reception. I look forward to meeting you individually over the next few weeks and hearing about your dioceses. This is a great occasion for Christianity to resolve the problems facing it. The unity of the Christian Church is imperative for peace and stability of the Roman Empire, as well as the growth of Christianity. I know you will embrace the issues facing you with honesty and good will. The emperor wishes to ensure your comfort and enjoy his hospitality." When she had finished she sat on the couch and again spoke to her slave.

Anastasia was just about to say something to her uncle when she felt someone touch her arm. She turned around and saw Valerius. Her joy immediately left her and was replaced with dread.

"What a pleasure to see you again," he said. "I would like to introduce you to the emperor's sister. You will enjoy her company." Without waiting for her reply he took her by the arm and led her to the platform. She tried to resist in a feeble way but his abrupt behavior left her speechless.

At the foot of the platform he bowed and spoke to the princess. "Your Highness, may I present Anastasia, niece of Bishop Caelius of Rome. She is active in her diocese and is of great help to her uncle."

Anastasia curtsied and lowered her head in reverence.

Constantia smiled and motioned her to come up to the platform.

E.D.S. SMITH

Anastasia stepped up and looked at the woman before her. She saw a woman with beautiful features but a blank expression. Her smile was hollow without emotion. Only her eyes spoke. They were sad, almost tragic.

"Anastasia, I welcome you to Nicaea and happy to see a woman amongst these holy men," she said pointing in the direction of the bishops. "We need more women leaders to reflect the Church's membership and devotion. Many women kept the Church alive when it was outlawed, and I hope the bishops do not forget it now that Christianity is legal. But I have my doubts and feel it will be a struggle." She waited for a moment to reflect on something and then said, "come sit by me and tell me about yourself."

Anastasia moved closer and as she did, she glanced at the slave. He had short black hair, almost shaved to the skin, the way slaves were required to wear. A high brow dominated his face and his dark eyes were set close together. His skin was olive and he was clean shaven. He looked not older than twenty five years. What was most noticeable about him were his hands. They were smooth with long fingers, his nails well maintained. It was evident he did not perform manual labor.

Their eyes met and a warm feeling came over Anastasia. She smiled at him but he did not return the smile, instead he quickly looked down on his tablet.

She was not offended. She knew that slaves were forbidden to socialize with guests unless permitted to do so. Even eye contact was punished if caught, and a smile could send him to the mines, a sure death. She shuddered as she always did when thinking of slavery, especially when it affected her personally, and this certainly did.

She sat next to Constantia and they began to chat about the trip, the life in Rome and life in the Eastern Empire. Anastasia described her early childhood and her present work at the diocese. "I teach the converts about Christianity and prepare them for baptism. I officiate at funerals and weddings and preach the Gospel to the congregation on Sundays. We feed the poor whose free rations are not always enough, and recently expanded our orphanage. Our doors are open to everyone, Christians, Jews, pagans, and anyone else who may knock on our door. This was the way of Christ."

Constantia listened with genuine interest. "I hope during your stay in Nicaea you will take time to relax and enjoy the lake and the beautiful surroundings that it offers. I can make arrangements for someone to take you around and show you the sights," she said. She looked at Valerius who was standing close by and added, "maybe Officer Valerius will do the honors."

Anastasia flinched but kept her wits about her. "Thank you most kindly, Your Highness, for your generous offer. I am reviewing the Gospels for passages that justify Jesus' Divinity and equality with the Father. I had promised my uncle to select verses that will defend our position as well as those the Arians will use to support their stand. For that reason I ask your permission to postpone your kind offer until I finish my work."

There was a moment of silence then Constantia spoke. "I applaud you, young lady, for your commitment to your work. I value this quality, unfortunately seldom found. We have a library here in Nicaea, not as big as the one in Alexandria or Constantinople, of course, but sufficiently equipped in old Christian and Jewish texts that may be helpful. Demetrius will assist you in finding the sources you seek." She pointed to the slave sitting behind her. "He is well educated, a trained librarian and a scholar of manuscripts. Our army captured him and others like him on the island of Crete during a revolt. He has been with us for several years."

Anastasia looked at Demetrius and saw him clench his fists. His face expressed resentment and shame. She felt pity for him, an educated Greek, once free and proud, and now reduced to a slave. Why?

"I will be most grateful to you for letting me use the library, and to Demetrius for helping me find the sources I need," she said, then looked at Demetrius with warmth.

"Then it's settled," Constantia said. "Whenever you are ready let Valerius know and he will make the arrangements. Demetrius belongs to Valerius but we share his intellect."

Valerius moved closer to Anastasia. He was smiling but his eyes were not. "I will make arrangements once I hear from you. I hope to see you very soon," he said kissing her hand.

She did not dare to pull away in front of Constantia. Instead she forced a smile.

He walked over to Demetrius and spoke. His demeanor was haughty and threatening. At one point he raised his fist to strike him then lowered it. Demetrius cowered but stood motionless ready to take the blow.

Anastasia felt as if his fist was aimed at her. She retired to her suite troubled and uneasy.

Chapter 9

The Council Begins, Late May A.D. 325

After several days of banquets and ceremonies where the bishops were treated to meals and delicacies which they never dreamed existed, as well as sightseeing and entertainment appropriate for bishops, it was time for the Council to begin.

On the eve of the Council Anastasia lay in bed thinking about the events to come. She had been granted permission to attend as Bishop Caelius' secretary, but it came with difficulties. There had been opposition because she was a woman, especially from some of the eastern bishops whose resistance to women's participation in the Church's business was strong. But Constantia intervened on her behalf and she was allowed to attend.

Among those hosting the bishops was Fausta the emperor's wife. It was common knowledge that she was haughty, conceited, and vulgar, who reveled in court intrigues. Yet her worst attribute was jealousy of anyone who she thought threatened her position or that of her sons, and she would go to any length to protect their status. She was a pagan and worshipped many gods, her favorite was Juno, the goddess of women and childbirth. Juno was the wife of Jupiter the king of gods, and her place among the goddesses was second to none. The emperor did not prevent her from worshipping the pagan gods, and gave her much leeway, perhaps because she had given him three sons and four daughters, ensuring his succession. She had considerable influence over her husband and could manipulate circumstances to her advantage, even to the point of life and death. Those at court knew that it was dangerous to be at odds with the empress.

The day the Council opened was a day full of anticipation and fanfare. A hall recently enlarged and refurbished was ready to accommodate about three hundred bishops. Bishop Caelius was one of the first to arrive, always preferring to be an hour early than a minute late. With Anastasia at his side wearing a long robe similar to the bishops' not to be conspicuous, and a notepad in hand, they entered the hall.

"It will be interesting how the Council decides the controversy of Jesus' Divinity," Bishop Caelius said turning to Anastasia. "Irrespective of the outcome, I'm afraid the conflict will linger for a long time after the Council is over, and Christian unity may be out of reach for generation, maybe even until the second coming of Christ." He stopped then added with sadness, "It is tragic that

Christians have been fighting amongst themselves almost since Jesus' death and continue to this day. They turn upon each other all in the name of Christ who taught peace."

The first thing that caught Anastasia's eye was the grandeur of the hall. Someone said it was called the Judgment Hall, and she wondered if that was where the emperor judged his subjects, sentenced them, and handed out punishments as the sole ruler of the empire. It was located in the palace proper, with an entrance that had two magnificent columns on each side made of white marble. The floor, also of marble, was yellow with violet and blue veins. Tall stained windows on three sides allowed colorful rays to illuminate the hall. Next to the windows, shining mosaics and frescos depicted Constantine's battles and conquests. In the middle of the hall stood a statue of Constantine seated on a throne holding an open Bible, representing himself as the thirteenth apostle. He had a crown on his head covered with jewels, and a halo above his head made of gold. This statue in particular struck Anastasia as arrogant, but she wouldn't have dared to say this, not even to her uncle. The emperor's presence was everywhere in the palace, revealing his need to show his power over everything including Christianity.

Fifteen rows of ascending benches were erected alongside three walls for the bishops to sit. Each row had fifty cushioned seats with backs upholstered in satin and brocade. Every seat had an attached folding table for bishops to take notes. Besides the bishops a substantial number of pagan scholars and priests of various religions were invited to contribute to the discussion.

As the bishops and guests filed in, pages escorted them to their seats. The seating was prearranged, the front rows and middle seats given to the most important bishops. Guests sat on the side rows. Anastasia and her uncle found themselves sitting in the middle of row six, with a good view of the podium from which the speakers would address the Council attendees.

"Uncle, I am a little tense now that it's all coming about," Anastasia said tugging at her uncle's sleeve. "I hope all goes well for us."

"Do not fret, my child. Trust in God. All is in His hands."

When everyone was inside, four slaves picked up the statue of Constantine and moved it slightly to the side but still within everyone's sight. A trumpet sounded from the corner of the hall and a hush fell over the audience. Everyone rose and fixed their eyes on the door. An officer with a plumed helmet carrying the imperial banner entered the hall.

There was something familiar about the officer. Anastasia felt uneasy. As he came closer she recognized Valerius. He was looking straight at her as if he had known where she would sit. A feeling of gloom came over her. He was everywhere, even here at the Council. Was he stalking her or was this a coincidence?

The trumpeter played again after which a courtier

dressed in a rich robe made the announcement. "Her Majesty, Empress Fausta, wife of Emperor Constantine." All eyes turned on her. She walked in slowly, holding her head high, turning from side to side, her expression severe and proud. The purple robe which she wore glittered with diamonds and rubies. Her high coiffure was arranged in curls sprinkled with pearls, to which was attached a gold veil with a long train attended by four young slave girls. A murmur arose amongst the bishops as they watched her. The glamor which she exuded left them in awe. She walked to a special chair apart from the bishops and sat down, her four slave girls trailing behind her.

Next came Constantia, the emperor's sister looking straight ahead. She equally sparkled in jewels, her silver robe swaying softly with two slave girls following behind. A transparent veil covered her face, a frozen mask without emotion. She walked gracefully to the side and sat next to the empress, the slave girls alongside of her. Behind her and carrying a tablet and a stylus came the slave Demetrius who placed himself next to Constantia. He was prepared to take notes of the proceedings. He wore a short blue tunic and leather sandals. Anastasia's eyes sparkled. What was it about him that attracted her to him? Could it be his intellect of which Constantia spoke so highly, or was it something else, or both?

After Constantia had made her entry, about twenty men some with long beards dressed in simple white robes walked in. Wooden crosses hung from their necks signifying their Christian faith. They were priests and monks who lived at the emperor's court and provided pastoral services to the court. They also instructed those who wished to convert from paganism to Christianity and prepared them for baptism. Military and court personnel and their families were especially eager to convert, sensing the new faith provided opportunities for advancement. After them came high ranking Roman officials in togas. They were followed by pagan officers in military uniforms who also served as pagan priests, and who have been invited to attend the Council and contribute when appropriate.

It was time for Emperor Constantine to enter the hall. Twelve trumpeters appeared in colorful tunics and played the victory song to which Constantine marched after his victory on the Milvian Bridge. Accompanying them were twelve vocalists who chanted the lyrics to the music praising Constantine as God's beloved. When they finished a high ranking official stepped forward and in a strong base made the announcement.

"His highest majesty, the noble, regal, magnificent, and anointed by the Christian God, Constantine, Emperor of the Roman Empire."

For a few moments all was still. Nobody made a sound. Then with measured steps the emperor entered the hall, his head tilted upward looking to heaven with an expression of piety and humility. His palms were folded in front of him and his lips were moving in silent prayer. On his head was a gold crown adorned with diamonds and pearls under which black locks were neatly arranged. He wore a silver robe from head to foot on which were sewn emeralds and sapphires. On the front of the robe designed with opal and turquoise stones was the symbol of a fish signifying the Christian theme, and the bottom of the robe green topaz and amethyst created a motif of sea and a boat.

Over his shoulders he wore a crimson cloak with gold embroidery, fastened in the front with a large ruby broach. A long train stretched behind him in folds, carried by four male slaves. In the back of the cloak superimposed upon each other in gold were the Greek capital letters XP, representing the first two letters for Christ.

After a few minutes, looking tall and majestic, he stepped to the podium and spoke. "Before we begin I ask my Christian envoy and bishop to lead us in prayer."

His envoy stood up and approached the podium. Raising his hands and looking up to heaven he led the bishops in reciting the Our Father. When finished he took out from his pocket a parchment and read a solemn invocation, calling on the Holy Spirit for divine blessing on the Council in resolving the issues at hand.

After a moment of silence the emperor addressed the bishops. "My dear Christian bishops of the Roman Empire, please sit down." He extended his arms in a gesture of welcome then waited until everyone was seated.

"I am pleased and grateful for your presence. I know that for many of you the journey was long, tiring, and dangerous. Yet in spite of it you left your diocese to resolve the most urgent matter facing Christianity. The questions you will have to answer are whether Jesus was the Only Begotten Son of God the Father, is of the same substance as the Father, and is co-eternal with the Father. Or was Jesus created by the Father from nothing, and sent to earth to save the world, and although perfect, is subordinate to the Father? In short, was Jesus born of the Father before all ages, true God from true God, equal to the Father, or not? It is not a simple matter, as you well know, and requires wisdom, knowledge of the Gospels, and inspiration of the Holy Spirit, of which I am confident you have all three."

He paused and motioned to a slave who immediately brought him a goblet from which he drank. After he had taken a few sips he was ready to proceed.

"Unfortunately there exists much hostility among the bishops who hold opposing views. These hostilities must be settled if Christianity is to survive. We cannot fight amongst ourselves and expect our flock to live true Christian lives. I say what is in my heart and I'm sure in yours, that peace and harmony must return to the Church. I urge you, bishops of the Roman Empire, to speak freely and express your views honestly, so that all sides would be heard and a right decision reached. I take no side and wish only that the truth emerge, and that you go home united."

He paused again, took few more swallows and closed his eyes as if to reflect, then continued, "I am also a bishop, appointed by God, and I came here to listen and learn from you. But I am your guest, so I humbly ask your permission to stay."

The bishops stood and began clapping and cheering, giving their approval for him to stay. At this point a courtier brought in a chair for the emperor and set it apart from the bishops, some distance from his wife and sister, yet close enough so he could hear the discussion and participate if he wished.

But on the spur of the moment, which often happened with the emperor, he approached the benches and began mingling with the bishops and greeting them individually. Most of them had scars from the persecutions, and as he walked from bench to bench and from bishop to bishop he asked about their wounds, their suffering and their survival. Approaching a lame bishop whose leg muscles were cut as punishment for not burning the Bible, he bent and massaged the bishop's legs and promised to provide him with a device that would help him walk. Seeing a bishop who lost his hand, he promised to send him an artificial hand.

Moving to the sixth row he saw Bishop Caelius and stopped in front of him. He looked with interest at the bishop's eye patch and asked how he lost his eye.

Bishop Caelius rose in respect and touched his patch a little self-conscious. "Your Majesty, I refused to sacrifice to the god Jupiter, so a soldier cut it out." He said no more not wishing to go into the details, partly because all this happened long ago and all was forgiven, and partly because he did not want to make the emperor feel guilty for something in which he took no part.

The emperor stood silent for a few moments then removed the patch form the bishop's eye and kissed his empty eye socket. "I will give you a crystal eye to match the color of your good eye," he said as he placed the patch back on the bishop's socket. "On second thought, I will give you several with different colors so you can change them at will."

Bishop Caelius murmured few words of thanks, and Anastasia curtsied and bowed her head in reverence. Both were astonished.

When he had finished talking to the bishops, the emperor approached the chair which was placed for him, and stood waiting for a signal from the presiding bishop to sit. The bishop motioned him to sit and he did, folding his hands on his knees.

At this time the presiding bishop stepped up to the podium. Gleaming with pleasure and bowing with deep respect he began to speak. "Your Majesty, we welcome you most heartily to this Council of bishops. You, who have been sent by God to deliver the Christians from persecutions and death have been our protector, our benefactor, and the one anointed by God to be our earthly savior. Without you the Christians would still be struggling and dying for their faith. You are God's representative on earth, and for your benevolence Christians will be forever grateful. You have honored us by this Council and by your presence here. We welcome you with all our hearts."

When he finished speaking all the bishops rose and clapped. Constantine stood up and bowed his head, his palms locked in prayer.

What followed were opening speeches by bishops representing the two opposing views. First to step up to the podium was a large man, about sixty years old, with a short beard and a head full of hair. He came from the eastern part of the empire and represented the faction that believed Jesus was subordinate to God the Father. As he spoke his thunderous voice resonated across the hall.

"My fellow bishops. We are here to discuss and settle what doctrine Christianity is to follow. You are well aware of the two opposing views: Is Jesus God and equal to God the Father or is he subordinate to the Father? Did Jesus always exist as a natural Son of the Father or was he created at some point by the Father?" He paused and took a sip of water. Before he continued speaking he glanced in the direction of the emperor who was listening attentively. "Many of us believe, including myself, that Jesus is not the natural son of God but was created by the Father out of nothing. That God the Father adopted him, gave him divine powers at some point and made him subordinate to God the Father. And even though he may have been created before the beginning of time, and was perfect, there was a time when Jesus did not exist, and only the Father existed. There is ample evidence in the Gospels, words spoken by Jesus himself that support this doctrine, and we will provide the proof in weeks ahead." He thanked the bishops for listening to him and sat down giving the floor to his opponent.

An elderly man in his seventies, with a long white beard and long white hair stepped up to the podium.

At that point Bishop Caelius leaned to Anastasia. "He is also from the Eastern Empire and holds an opposing view, our view, that Jesus is God and equal to God the Father. I met him a few times and he's a nice chap, but his young assistant is brutal in enforcing his views on the populace. I disagree with his tactics and strongly condemn them. Not the way of Christ," he said.

"My fellow bishops," the speaker began. "What my opponent said is heresy. The Gospels will show that Jesus had always existed and was sent by the Father to redeem the world. He is the natural Son of God, the Only Begotten Son the Father, and not created as my opponent claims. He is of the same substance as the Father, equal to God the Father and the Holy Spirit. He is a member of the Trinity." Having said what he wanted he looked at the emperor who was nodding his head.

Anastasia listened attentively then turned to her uncle. "These bishops are making their cases but they speak to impress the emperor rather than their fellow bishops. I feel the emperor may be the final arbiter."

"You may be right, my child. It may very well be that the emperor will decide."

It was time for a lunch, and the bishops walked to the

atrium where a magnificent meal awaited them. The elderly and lame were led to the couches where they reclined in
comfort, the rest were seated on soft chairs. Slaves moved
silently among them serving food and drink.

Anastasia guided her uncle to a couch and was about
to sit by him when she saw Constantia, the emperor's sister
across the room. With her was Demetrius. Her eyes flashed.
Something prompted her to approach them. She excused
herself and made her way towards them losing her shy-
ness. "Your Highness, you had allowed me to use the library.
May I have your permission to use it today? " She glanced
at Demetrius whose head was tilted downward yet his eyes
were raised in her directions. They were inquiring and kind.

"Of course my dear." Turning to Demetrius she said,
"take Lady Anastasia to the library today at her conve-
nience and help her locate the materials she needs."

Demetrius turned to Anastasia. "I am at your disposal.
With your permission I will wait for you in the atrium following the meeting."

Anastasia thanked him and was about to join her uncle when someone touched her on shoulder from behind.
Before she turned around she knew who it was.

"My lady, I couldn't help but overhear," Valerius said
speaking to Anastasia but looking at Constantia. "I will
take the liberty to join you in the library myself and meet
you there after the Council meeting. There is much that
I can learn, besides, being with you will give me much
pleasure."

"As you wish Valerius," Constantia said taken aback and showing her displeasure. With that she left and motioned Demetrius to follow.

Anastasia could only listen but inside she was furious. What right did he have to intrude? What right did he have to touch her? She glared at Valerius aware that her feelings were showing, but didn't care.

She walked back to her uncle, angry tears blurring her vision. Will he ever leave her alone or would she have to take steps to stop him?

Chapter 10

Anastasia did not eat lunch having lost her appetite after the encounter with Valerius. She went back to the Council but left early. She wanted to see Demetrius alone before Valerius arrived and she hadn't much time.

Passing through a large hallway she turned a corner and entered a garden surrounded on all sides by Grecian columns. How beautifully landscaped the garden was she thought, looking at the flowers, the bushes, and a large fountain in the middle with cherubims sprouting pink water to the skies. The gravel paths weaving through the garden were bordered with pink marble, and alongside stood busts of famous Roman generals. A sole statue was that of Constantine on a horse, waving his sword in one hand and in the other holding a cross. Every fifty paces stood benches in the shape of sea shells with canopies to shield from the sun, providing rest or a place to talk with companions.

Leaving the garden she came to a large building in front of which was a portico with more Grecian columns.

Walking into the building she found herself in a large hall the likes of which she had never seen before. Against three walls from the bottom to the top were built- in- shelves, some small and others large, some vertical and others horizontal in which books and scrolls were neatly filed. In the middle of the room were long tables with benches, which Anastasia assumed were for serious scholars. On the sides of the room were comfortable chairs and couches for those who read for pleasure. Three slaves stood watch in the room to assist the readers and to prevent theft and vandalism to the books.

Rays of sunlight came through a glass ceiling during the day to all corners of the library, while in the evening slaves lit candles and candelabra in close proximity to tables and chairs. Leading from the far corner was a separate room with comfortable seating and a table with sweets and wine. This was the place where patrons could socialize and discuss events of the day, since it was forbidden to speak in the library and silence was strictly enforced.

Anastasia's eyes circled the room, and in the corner of the library surrounded by scrolls and bent over a manuscript she saw Demetrius. He was intensely absorbed in what he was reading and did not see her until she stood beside him.

"Forgive me my lady. I did not expect you so soon." He jumped to his feet and looked nervously around him. "Did Officer Valerius come with you?"

"No, I wanted to see you alone." She hesitated what

to say next, but her lips moved easily. "I did not want him with me. I would like to work only with you, if I may."

"My lady this is your choice and certainly it would be mine, but I have nothing to say in this matter. I am a slave and do what I'm told. If I were a free man I would….." he did not finish, instead his face took on a frightened expression as he listened to approaching footsteps.

Within moments they found themselves face to face with Valerius. It was a face that Anastasia had not seen before. His eyes narrow and cold, his lips bent in a downward curve, he exuded rage that was real and frightening. In his hand he held a whip. For a moment Anastasia felt threatened for her own safety, but what he did next was not aimed at her.

With a violent thrust and a fierce cry of fury he raised his arm and swung the whip heavy on the back of Demetrius. The force of the whip swept Demetrius sideways, who fell to the floor several paces away. He rose slowly and leaned against the wall shaking.

Anastasia was in shock. She ran to Demetrius and stood in front of him shielding him from further beating, and cried out her voice shaking. "How dare you do this? I will report you to Her Highness. You are not allowed to mistreat slaves. I know the law."

Valerius' tone was arrogant, his reply curt. "My lady, I regret that you witnessed this, but may I inform you that Demetrius is my slave and under my command. He does what I tell him. Her Highness Constantia utilizes him for his scholarly knowledge with my permission. He has disobeyed me and received just punishment."

"How did he disobey you?" She asked her eyes flashing with rage.

"I am not required to justify my actions but nevertheless I will tell you. He spoke to you without my permission."

"He was not at fault. I was the one that initiated the conversation."

"He knows what to do in these cases."

"I saw other slaves speak at will with the guests."

"They were given permission. Owners of slaves set their own rules."

Anastasia had never experienced the anger she felt towards him at that moment. He disgusted and repulsed her not only by his brutality which he now showed, but by his boldness towards her. His aggression had no limits and his rank allowed him to do what he liked. She had not complained about him so far, but now she must speak out. But to whom? Would her uncle understand and challenge Valerius on personal matters? She wasn't sure. She glanced at Demetrius who by now stopped shaking and stood silently waiting for orders. Yet his face was proud. Her heart went out to him. She must find a way to reach him without jeopardizing his safety or hers.

Valerius walked over to Demetrius and spoke to him, then came back and faced Anastasia. His voice now was soft, almost a whisper. "Demetrius is ready to offer assistance. Please provide him with your questions and he will supply the necessary sources."

Anastasia tried to collect her thoughts but the violent scene prevented her from thinking. "Sir, I will return another time."

She started to leave when Valerius stopped her. "There's no better time than now. Demetrius had already spread out the sources and they are waiting for your perusal. I will stay nearby and escort you back to your quarters when you are finished."

She saw him sit on a chair his eyes focused on her. Feeling trapped and angry, she nevertheless walked to a table where the Bible and various manuscripts were neatly displayed. Demetrius stood ready to help her. She turned to him and a feeling of warmth embraced her. "I would like to review the passages from the Gospels proclaiming Christ as God. Today I'll begin with the Gospel according to John."

Demetrius picked up the Gospel and opened it to Chapter 1, Verse 1 'This may be the start of your search," he said. "*In the beginning was the Word, and the Word was with God, and the Word was God. He was in the beginning with God. All things came to be through him, and without him nothing came to be. What came to be through him was life, and this life was the light of the human race;..... And the Word became flesh and made his dwelling among us, and we saw his glory the glory of the Father's only Son full of grace and truth.*"

Reading further in John, Chapter 14, Verse 9. "*..... Whoever has seem me has seen the Father. ......The Father who* *dwells in me is doing his works. Believe me that I am in the Father and the Father is in me, or else, believe because of the works themselves."*

She knew these verses by heart but today they were especially relevant. Jesus preexisted as the Word of God and assumed human form in the person of Jesus Christ, revealing the Father to us. Jesus was, is, and always will be God, literally. And in John's Chapter 14, Jesus himself reaffirmed that he is one with the Father.

But she knew that the Arians would see it differently. To them the same passages could mean something else. That Jesus although being the Word, and made divine at some point, who came down to earth to save humanity, was not of the same substance or identical to the Father, and not equal to God the Father.

Next, Demetrius held a book containing the New Testament Letters. He opened the page to St. Paul's Letter to the Colossians.

Anastasia knew St. Paul's words of the Person and Work of Christ, and read starting at Chapter 1, Verse 15. *"He is the image of the invisible God, the firstborn of all creation. For in him were created all things in heaven and on earth, the visible and the invisible, whether thrones or dominions or principalities or powers; all things were created through him and for him......"*

But Arius again would argue that *"All things were created through him,"* could mean that Jesus was given the power to create by God the Father, as a superior would give authority to the subordinate. Therefore Jesus was inferior to God the Father. In the final analysis Arius would argue that Jesus was created and was not the Creator.

She returned to John's Chapter 14, Verse 28 where Jesus said "..... *I am going away and I will come back to you. If you loved me you will rejoice that I am going to the Father; For the Father is greater than I." And Verse 31 ".....I love the Father and that I do just as the Father has commanded me. ....."*

Was Jesus inferior by his own words? Certainly not. By becoming human for a short time Jesus did not lose or relinquish his Divinity. When conceived in Mary's womb by the Holy Spirit, He acquired human nature and still remained God. He became obedient to God the Father as the rest of humanity. He placed himself in a lesser position and submitted to God the Father, doing His will. But He was, is, and always will be God.

The letter to the Hebrews, Chapter 2, Verse 9 explains that. ". ... *but we do see Jesus crowned with glory and honor because he suffered death, he who for a little while was made lower than the angels, that by the grace of God he might taste death for everyone."*

St. Paul further clarifies the two natures of Jesus, divine and human in his letter to the Philippians, Chapter 2, Verse 5. "*Have among yourselves the same attitude that is also yours in Christ Jesus, Who, though he was in the form of God, did not regard equality with God something to be grasped. Rather he emptied himself, taking the form of a slave, coming in human likeness; and found human in appearance, he humbled himself, becoming obedient to death, even death on a cross.......and every tongue confesses that Jesus Christ is Lord, to the glory of God the Father."*

Anastasia felt satisfied that every effort to discredit Jesus as being God, Arius and his followers would be met by an aggressive rebuttal.

The day was coming to a close as she finished her work for the day with Demetrius by her side, and the harsh gaze of Valerius from the distance. She was amazed at Demetrius' knowledge of the Scriptures. She wondered if he was a Christian. Probably not, but as a scholar he had studied Christianity. When handing him back the books her hand touched his hand. It was warm and tender. Their eyes met and spoke. When they parted both knew something remarkable was emerging between them.

Chapter 11

It was evening and Demetrius, his work finished for the day, walked towards the slave quarters, a building next to the palace. It had recently been remodeled with fresh paint inside and out, and modern sanitary fixtures installed, not for the slaves' sake, but to control the putrid odor. Inside he passed a room with straw mattresses where lower ranking slaves slept, then walking through a long corridor entered a room with beds, dressers and shelves where slaves of higher ranking like him called home. He occupied the best section of the room, in the far corner, with the closest fellow slave several feet away. It was a comfortable abode as slave quarters go, with fresh water available from a cistern, and a commode almost as modern as those in the palace proper. To the left of him was a window, where he spent few precious minutes every day looking out and dreaming of life when he was free.

He was born on the Greek island of Crete, which became part of the Roman Empire when the Roman legions swept through the barrier islands. His parents were free

Greeks whose values centered on scholarship and learning. His mother received a good education that was normally given only to boys. When Demetrius and his sister were born, she made sure that they were educated, and encouraged them to use their intellect to the fullest. His father was a teacher to children of prosperous inhabitants of the island, and Demetrius often went with him to hear the lessons and play with his pupils. Not far from their home was the local library, and when Demetrius wasn't busy, he could be found in the library reading old manuscripts.

When he became a teenager, his parents sent him to college to finish his education. He studied the arts, philosophy, and the sciences which qualified him to pursue a career in law, science or administration. Yet to nobody's surprise he chose to become a librarian, and after graduation served as assistant librarian in the library where he once read as a boy. His sister who studied mathematics became an accountant to a local exporting firm that did business with the Romans.

Although the Romans ruled the Greek island, life was good for free Greeks. Most free Greeks had slaves as did his parents, and at the time he thought nothing of it. In the community where he lived people were not rich, but life was filled with lectures, picnics, swimming in the ocean and attending the theater. Everything he loved and wanted was on the island he called home. The mountains, valleys, the rivers and the sea, and the animals and plants gave him a feeling of freedom and appreciation for nature.

His favorite pastime was bird watching with his friends. He loved the birds and agonized when hunters pointed their arrows at them.

Then suddenly everything changed. A small insurrection erupted on the island against the Romans. The insurgents had no chance of winning and were quickly defeated, but Roman vengeance did not stop there. Not only did they execute the rebels who took part in the revolt, but enslaved the whole population of the island, and took many of the people as slaves to Rome and other parts of the empire. His mother died a slave on a distant island soon after capture, and his father died of fever before being shipped to Italy. Demetrius and his sister were taken to Rome to be sold on the auction block. Put in chains in horrible conditions, and given only enough food and water to survive, he came to know the evils of slavery. He recalled the slaves that his family owned and tried to remember how they were treated. His mind was blank and maybe just as well. He did not wish to remember.

On the long and brutal sea journey his sister died. Demetrius grieved for her, and yet it was a comfort to him that she escaped the terrible fate of a Roman female slave.

He remembered how humiliated he felt when a slave trader grilled him on his education and skills, then ordered him to strip naked. On the auction block he put a sign around his neck that read "educated Greek, reads and writes Greek and Latin, librarian by profession." He stood with his eyes fixed to the ground, his fists clenched, boiling with rage and humiliation, wanting to die. He was not long on the block. A Roman officer bought him on his first bid. It was Valerius. Within minutes as fate would have it, Constantia, the emperor's sister drove by in her litter and offered him twice the amount he paid. To his great misfortune Valerius refused, but loaned him to her. This was his status with which he lived. His stay in Rome was short. Valerius was transferred to the Eastern Empire and took Demetrius with him.

Tonight he was tired and reaching his cot lay down hoping for sleep. Some of his fellow slaves had already retired. Among them was his good friend, Arbeas, a talented sculptor from a neighboring Greek island with many years in captivity. Arbeas had the good fortune to belong to an aristocratic Roman lady who was a patron of arts and who valued his talents. He sculpted for her family and she treated him with kindness and respect. Recently she loaned him to the emperor to sculpt a bust of his oldest son Crispus, so he moved from her villa to the palace. Having been a trusted slave for a long time, he enjoyed fine food and clothing, and liberty leaves to town. His owner paid him wages, as was sometimes done to trusted slaves.

It was getting late and Demetrius had closed his eyes when someone nudged him on the shoulder. He looked up and saw Arbeas. "I want to share good news with you, at least it's good news for me," Arbeas said with a little guilt. "I have saved enough money to buy my freedom and will be leaving soon. My mistress arranged for me to teach sculpting at the school of the arts. The position comes with good pay and a comfortable apartment. I will be a free man," he said unable to contain his joy.

"I will miss you my dear friend," Demetrius said wishing it could be him.

"There will be a ceremony celebrating my freedom. My mistress arranged that I be granted Roman citizenship. I am most grateful to her. With the money I saved I will have enough to buy my sweetheart's freedom too. We will be married soon after."

"I rejoice in your happiness," Demetrius said knowing of the love shared between his friend and a slave girl in the same household.

A moment of silence and then Arbeas spoke somewhat embarrassed. "Here I am sharing my joy with you. How insensitive of me."

"Do not be concerned. I know my destiny. I will die a miserable slave. There is no hope for me. Valerius will not sell me to another master, neither will he pay me wages so I can buy my freedom. I am doomed."

"I wish I could help you but my situation is fragile. My help could jeopardize my freedom. We all know the true nature of Valerius. He could stop my release with false accusations even if I don't belong to him. But once I'm free I will ask my mistress to intervene to the emperor on your behalf." He felt remorseful and his face showed it.

"Do not feel guilty my friend. I will take what comes," Demetrius said. He settled down in his cot and his thoughts turned to Anastasia. There was something special about the girl. A bond had formed between them. But why? He was a pagan slave from Greece, and she was a Roman citizen and a Christian. By all measures he should be hostile, instead he felt warmth towards her. It was more than that. His feelings were sensuous. He recalled her eyes as she gazed at him. Did she feel the same way? He shook his head as if to purge the thought. He must not dare to think of the unthinkable, and yet it gave him comfort.

Chapter 12

Several days had passed and the Council had pro-
gressed at the expected speed. The discussions, sometimes emotional and explosive, sometimes calm and ratio-
nal, took up most of the days, with both sides seeking the
inspiration of the Holy Spirit and reading the Gospel but
understanding it differently. Anastasia dutifully listened to
all that was said, took notes and passed them to her hard
of hearing uncle. She worked and studied, and in her free
time she thought of Demetrius.

On one occasion when the Arians introduced false
claims denying the Trinity and the Divinity of Jesus, her
uncle, who usually controlled his anger, stood up trembling, unable to suppress it. His face red and his eyes moist,
his voice the pinnacle of emotion, he recited Jesus' words
to his disciples after His Resurrection, according to the
Gospel of Matthew, Chapter 28, Verse 18. *".... All power
in heaven and on earth has been given to me. Go, therefore,
and make disciples of all nations, baptizing them in the name
of the Father, and of the Son, and of the Holy Spirit, teaching*

them to observe all that I have commanded you. And behold, I am with you always, until the end of the age." When he had finished and felt he had said enough, a force within him urged him to continue. He turned to Arius and asked with a softer tone, "do you not see the meaning of Jesus' words? Jesus commanded his disciples to baptize in the name of the Father, the Son, and the Holy Spirit, identifying the three person, equal in Divinity. By saying *'in the name'* and not 'in the names', Jesus united them in one God, the Trinity."

He sat down, sweat on his brow, more sad than angry at the shallowness and ignorance of some of the bishops.

Anastasia wiped her uncle's brow and settled him down, reminding him not to get excited. Seeing that he was comfortable she took a few minutes of rest in the shadows of the palace garden behind a bush. She was thinking of Demetrius when she saw Princess Constantia appear. She was by herself and did not see her. After looking around and thinking she was alone, the princess found a bench and covering her face with her hands began to cry.

Anastasia did not know if she should approach her or not, but her sobs were so pitiful that she felt she must do something. She walked towards the woman and said softly, "Your Highness, may I help in some way?"

Constantia raised her head and with a look of embarrassment waived her hands as if there was nothing wrong. But within a moment she was sobbing again.

Anastasia took the liberty of sitting beside her, even though the protocol dictated she should be asked. She wrapped her arm around the woman's shoulders as one woman comforting another and waited.

What seemed like a long time during which Constantia wiped her tears and straightened her robe, she took Anastasia's hand and said, "forgive me for making a scene. Nobody sees me cry, not even my ladies in waiting or my intimate slaves. I cry alone but today my grief came suddenly and I could not suppress it."

"Grief?" Anastasia dared to ask.

"My grief is linked to a secret that nobody speaks about at court. A secret so terrible that it is forbidden on penalty of treason to bring it up."

"Treason?"

"Yes, treason. My lips should be sealed but I feel that I can trust you, even though I had known you only a short time."

"Your Highness, I will not betray you."

Constantia sat silent for a long time. Her eyes looked to the distance and her face showed agony and resignation. "Today is my young son's birthday. He would have been ten years old. He died a tragic death, less than a year ago, and when he died so did I."

"Died?"

"Yes, murdered, together with my husband Licinius. Both strangled in their beds, both when asleep." Her voice became shrill, uncontrollable, and hysterical. For a moment

Anastasia thought she would scream but she settled down and began sobbing again.

"Who murdered them?"

"One of royal blood."

"Royal blood?"

"My brother, the emperor ordered their murder."

"Why?" Anastasia asked aghast.

"He thought they threatened his throne and would overthrow him but it wasn't true. When my husband Licinius lost the civil war against him, I went to my brother and begged him for mercy which he gladly offered. After all, I was his sister and I loved my husband. He forgave Licinius and promised he would be safe. My husband retired from politics and he, I, and our son went to live in the country. We were happy away from the court, living in our villa, entertaining our friends and enjoying a peaceful life." She paused as more sobs interrupted her. "But intrigues got the better of the emperor. My husband's enemies conspired against him, and persuaded the emperor that he was a threat." She again began to sob and pressed her hands to her heart "Oh, if only I hadn't left. If I had been by their side this wouldn't have happened. You see, I was away from home, that's when the killers did their evil deed."

"But the boy," Anastasia said. "What harm could he do?"

"Old men die and younger ones replace them. My brother eliminated the line, never to pose a threat to him or his sons. But my son didn't have to die. He was no threat to the crown and never would have been. He was gentle and loving and a talented artist, even at the young age. He wanted to paint and carve and not be a soldier. He hated war and killing." She pulled from her neck a gold chain to which was attached a wooden locket with a painting of a woman embracing a boy. "He made this for me before he was murdered. This I will wear to my grave." She again broke into sobs.

"But you were his sister, your son was his nephew. How could this happen?"

"You do not know the greedy and powerful that inhabit the court. Yes, I was his sister and my son was his nephew. He played with him, took him on trips and gave him gifts. He was more than an uncle. He was a second father to him. He used to say that himself. But that made no difference when it came to ambition. Greed and lust for power trumped all. Distrust and suspicion justified the deed. The threat of losing his throne, unfounded as it was, drove him to murder two innocent people, and one of them a little boy."

"How does he reconcile murder with Christianity which he embraced?"

Constantia laughed, a hollow and sarcastic laugh. "He has not yet been baptized and will not until near death. The bishops tell him that baptism forgives and erases all sins, so his soul is pure and enters immediately God's Kingdom. A dying man has no time to sin. He will go straight to heaven if he sins no more." She paused and sighed. "And my brother has still more sins to commit to secure his empire. Baptism will have to wait."

"How could he face you after what he did?"

"He felt remorse for giving me grief but not for what he did. He is beyond that. He gave me jewels, slaves, and villas to expunge his guilt and buy my forgiveness. And he achieved both. He erased his guilt and I have forgiven him, but not for the gifts he gave me. I am a Christian and had to forgive. But I am a shadow, a ghost of who I once was. I am dead inside."

Anastasia recalled her tragic eyes when the first time she saw her. Now she understood.

Constantia continued. "Be careful of the people at court. Don't trust anyone until you are sure. Be leery of Valerius. He is ambitious and dangerous. He is also powerful and my brother's confidante. I do not trust him. He has destroyed many who had crossed his path. I have no proof but I believe he was behind my husband and son's murder." She took hold of Anastasia's hand and said, "I think you appeal to him. Whether that pleases you or not I do not know. You must be the judge. But beware of him." She rose and gave a bitter laugh. "I must go now and pretend all is well. Oh, I'm good at that. I will see you soon, perhaps on a happier note."

"Your Highness, I have a favor to ask you. I hesitate to broach it but….."

"Speak up my child."

"I wish to use the library without Valerius present."

Constantia looked intensely at her and read her mind. "I will try to help." With that she took her leave.

Anastasia watched the tragic figure disappear from view. Constantia's story affected her deeply. A woman burdened with sorrow and guilt yet kindness in her heart. A rarity in the world of violence.

Chapter 13

In the days that followed Anastasia kept busy, attending the Council and visiting the library where Demetrius provided the sources she needed. Valerius was present most of the time, but even when away, they dared not speak unless it related to work. They knew that if caught Demetrius would suffer. Yet she wanted to know his past, his home, and what he did before enslavement. She yearned to hear his hopes, joys, grief, and despair. In spite of the silence the bond between them grew, and their eyes conveyed what was in their hearts.

One day an opportunity presented itself, yet with it came a blow for which she was unprepared. She was sitting in the garden enjoying a moment when she saw Valerius approaching her. It was too late to leave. He sat beside her and spoke to the point. His voice was smooth and the tone was friendly.

"The emperor is sending me to quell a revolt in one of our outposts. It's a small rebellion so I shall not be long. In the meantime, I have something important to tell you." He waited for her reaction and since none came he continued. "I have spoken to the emperor of my intentions and he has approved." He paused to choose his words, then with a soft voice and a caring look he said, "I love you and want to marry you. I will be a good husband and will make you happy." He waited for her to say something but she was speechless. Finally he reached for her hand and kissing it said, "will you accept me?"

Anastasia was numb, unable to withdraw her hand. Her lips moved but no words came out. When she found her voice her words were slow and measured. "Sir, it is not possible. I could not accept."

"Why?" He looked surprised. "I am a Christian, a Roman, and my career as a commander is ensured. My fortune is growing, and even today I am considered a wealthy man."

"I do not love you."

"Love? Is that important?"

"For me it is."

"You will grow to love me as I love you."

"I will never love you. My answer is no."

"I will give you jewels, slaves, and a magnificent villa." His voice became urgent.

"They mean nothing to me. I am not for sale."

"I am not buying you. Your words offend me."

"I am sorry. It was not my intent."

"What can I say to have you agree?"

"Nothing. The answer is no, today, tomorrow, and forever."

Hearing her answer his demeanor changed. His eyes narrowed and his lips tightened. His face took on an arrogant look. With a harsh voice he said, "I have made up my mind and will not give you up."

"You will have to, for I will never be your wife."

For a moment neither spoke. Valerius clenched his fists. Anastasia stared into the distance, composed.

"I will see you when I return. By then you will feel differently." With that he rose, bowed, and left.

Anastasia watched him leave. Her eyes were blurred, her head was spinning. She began to lose her composure. Feeling weak she leaned against the bench. For a moment she thought she would faint, but strength returned and with it resolve. She will die before marrying Valerius.

Chapter 14

Anastasia had not spoken to anyone about Valerius' proposal of marriage and struggled what to do about it. She wondered if she should tell her uncle, but decided against it for now, not wishing to worry him. Much work remained at the Council yet, and he needed freedom from personal problems. Grateful for Valerius' absence and excited at being alone with Demetrius, she wondered if Constantia had arranged his trip. True, a rebellion was brewing in the west, but a low ranking officer usually squelched minor revolts.

The sun was setting as she made her way to the library, knowing that Demetrius would soon be leaving. Today they would be alone and her spirits were high. She spotted him in the corner putting the parchments back on the shelves. When he saw her coming his eyes lit, yet he did not step forward.

Sensing his caution she hurried to him. "Do not worry. Valerius is away and we are alone."

They gazed at each other not knowing what to say.

Anastasia took the lead. "So far our eyes have spoken but now our lips can speak." She wanted to tell him what was in her heart, instead she said, "I want to thank you for helping me."

"I am at your disposal, my lady." His heart was racing and he reached out to touch her, but pulled back.

"Call me Anastasia," she said.

"It's a beautiful name and means resurrection in Greek," he said.

"My mother named me in honor of Christ."

A moment of silence and Anastasia continued. "There is something I want to tell you. I am in despair. I need a friend that I can trust."

"I will never betray you," Demetrius said.

"It's Valerius. He wants to marry me and the emperor has approved."

"Do you love him?" Demetrius asked after a long pause.

"No. If there is such thing as hate I am very close to it."

"In that case refuse him. You are free and in charge of your destiny. Use your freedom which I do not have. I am a slave and my master controls me," he said with bitterness.

"I refused him but he insisted."

"Speak to your uncle. He is a bishop and carries weight. The emperor will understand."

"Perhaps."

They left the library and walked to the garden, passing a fountain with Apollo, the sun god, sprouting water from his brow in the form of sun rays. Finding a bench they sat down. The fragrance of the garden captured Anastasia's senses and for a moment she forgot her troubles.

"Where is your homeland," she asked.

"Greece, the island of Crete. Once a beautiful place, now a heap of rubble. After the revolt the Romans destroyed everything and took most citizen slaves. I am the only one in my family who survived. My parents and sister perished."

Anastasia bowed her head. Again the evils of slavery stirred within her. "Did you take part in the revolt?" she asked.

"No, neither did my family but Rome's vengeance extended to all."

Anastasia didn't know what made her do it, but she reached to Demetrius and kissed him on the lips. Realizing what she had done she pulled back abruptly, and flung her hands over her mouth. "I'm sorry, forgive me."

Startled, Demetrius touched his lips, tears filling his eyes. With trembling voice he said, "there is nothing to forgive. Your kiss was the sweetest thing since I became a slave. I will cherish it forever."

Recovering from her boldness Anastasia sensed a feeling of pleasure which she had not felt before. Her lips on his aroused her. It frightened her, but she didn't want it to go away.

In parting Demetrius took her hand and kissed it. For one brief moment since his enslavement he felt like a man. The invisible chains dropped. He was no longer a slave but a man desiring a woman.

He walked to his quarters sensing the change within him. He had been dead but now was alive. Will he stop there or will he reach for things forbidden?

That night Demetrius tossed in bed with Anastasia's images before him. Was he in love or was it an illusion? Was he feeling gratitude to a girl who had shown him kindness, or was his heart aflame with something else? Before enslavement no girl evoked the same emotions. Anastasia aroused his passions. His manhood erupted and took over his being. The energy within him exploded. But what would become of it all? Was there a future? Or was the future only in his dreams?

And what about Anastasia? His thoughts took him further. Why did she kiss him? What did it mean? Was it compassion for a slave who would never be free, or was it a sign of something else? He didn't know but his soul awakened and his heart sang.

Anastasia walked towards her quarters with her heart aroused. Was she falling in love, a forbidden love that would lead to heartache? That night as she lay in bed, an image of Demetrius appeared before her. He was standing on a mountain top, free and proud, sending her kisses and beckoning her to come. Was that the future? She didn't dare to hope. It was only her dream.

Chapter 15

As days passed Anastasia found joy being with Demetrius, yet her anguish increased waiting for Valerius. Reluctant to worry her uncle yet needing to share his plans of marriage, she made a decision to tell him. Her opportunity came one morning as they walked to the Council together.

"Did Valerius speak to you about me before he left?" she asked him cautiously.

The bishop looked at her surprised. "No, my child. Should he have?"

Anastasia hesitated not knowing how to proceed. She decided that truth and candor were best. Taking in a deep breath she said, "he wants to marry me. I don't know how else to say it."

The startled bishop stopped walking. Seeing a bench nearby he sat down. "And how do you feel about it?" he finally uttered.

"Uncle, I could never marry him and I told him so. I do not love him. But the emperor approved and Valerius insisted."

"Then it's settled my child," he said firmly. "No one will force you to marry against your will. It's against our Christian faith. I will speak to the emperor about it. "

"He was very persistent," Anastasia said. "I hope this will not cause you problems, dear uncle."

The bishop looked at her kindly and for a moment saw her mother in her.

"You have your mother's passionate heart and her resolve," the bishop said with nostalgia. "Your mother loved your father the moment she saw him, and no reasoning would change her mind. I tried to tell her the problems of marrying a pagan, but it did no good. She replied that love would conquer all. And so it did in her case. Your father loved your mother, and even though a pagan, respected her faith and was sympathetic to it. Had he lived he may have converted but to your mother it made no difference."

"I want to marry for love but I also want to impact our growing Christian Church."

"Yes, my dear. Your mother lives in you. I know your wishes and I pray they will be fulfilled. The Church is growing, evolving and defining itself, and addressing many challenges. Look at the controversy of the Divinity of Jesus. It is only the beginning what the Church will face. More challenges will come and the Church will need bright minds to resolve them. I hope there is room for women to be leaders and ministers of the Church.

Since the early days of Christianity the women have served admirably. But I'm afraid this is dwindling and a new order will follow. It is sad that since Christianity became legal, women have been pushed aside and men have taken over. But some day women will serve the Church as priests and bishops, not in my lifetime, and not for a long time, but some day, I firmly believe it. God gave women intellect equal to men, and as mothers they have compassion and patience. It is wrong to waste God's gifts."

She loved when her uncle spoke like this. He was her advocate, all women's advocate. "I believe the Bible identifies women ministers," Anastasia said trying to remember.

"Just read St. Paul's Letter to the Romans, Chapter 16, Verse 1," the bishop said. "*I commend to you Phoebe our sister, who is also a minister of the church at Cenchreae, that you may receive her in the Lord in a manner worthy of the holy ones, and help her in whatever she may need from you, for she has been a benefactor to many and to me as well.*"

After reflecting a few minutes the bishop continued. "During the persecutions your mother had more authority than the women serving the Church today. I am convinced that if we had women bishops today, our problems would be lesser and more readily resolved. Women would bring order and calmness to handling disputes. Mind you, they can also be tough and persistent, which your mother was when needed."

He reflected again then said what has always given him shame. "It is tragic that Mary Magdalene, one of Jesus' disciples, who stayed with Jesus to the end while others fled, a holy woman with deep spirituality, was defamed by the Church. She should have been a leader and model for others, instead the Church unjustly, without any proof, incriminated her as a prostitute, then made a penitent saint of her."

"Do you think her reputation will be restored," Anastasia asked.

The bishop thought for a long time. "I believe the Church will exonerate her. The truth must be revealed. The Church made mistakes and will make them in the future, but if the Church repents and rectifies the mistakes, God will forgive. You must remember that the people make the Church, and people are sinners."

Anastasia listened attentively, and when the bishop finished she was more determined than ever to work for the Church. She took her uncle's hands between hers, and squeezing them tightly said what was in her heart. "In spite of the biases and inequality shown to women today, and the work that has been taken away from us, I am glad that I'm a woman. It may take a long time for the Church to accept and value us as ministers, but the world changes, and a time will come when the pope and the bishops will welcome women to the full service of God."

The bishop nodded, proud of his niece.

Anastasia took her uncle by the arm and they walked

together to the Council. He had given his approval for rejecting Valerius for which she was grateful, and which gave her courage. She would tell him about Demetrius at another time. There was no reason to complicate matters now.

Chapter 16

Days of the Council continued, and Anastasia, although immersed in the Council's proceedings, found time to meet with Demetrius. In Valerius' absence their feelings intensified and blossomed into love. As soon as the meetings were over, she rushed to the library to be with Demetrius. Her eyes sparkled, her face flushed as she melted in his embrace. He waited for her with impatience not knowing if she would come, and when she did, flung his arms around her and kissed her with passion. They nurtured their love, living for each other, oblivious to the dangers around them and the one that would betray them.

They spoke of the future and their life together. Their plan took shape. With her uncle's help the emperor would release her from marrying Valerius. They would plead for Demetrius' freedom and together work for Rome and the Christian Church.

Captivated with love, Demetrius' bleak existence changed to hope and courage. His once bitter heart filled with joy, and his somber soul began to live. His happiness was bursting within him, and he had to share it with someone.

One evening inside his quarters he approached his fellow slave Arbeas. "A wonderful thing happened to me. I am in love," he said with radiance.

"In love?" Arbeas said.

"Yes, love."

"Who is she?" he asked with genuine curiosity.

"I dare not say, and yet I will tell you because I trust you. I cannot contain my joy anymore and must say what's in my heart. It's Anastasia, a bishop's niece. We love each other."

Arbeas froze. His eyes which have been smiling showed fear. He spoke slowly, his tone severe. "You've broken the law. The penalty for socializing with a free woman is torture and the mines. You may even be killed if Valerius has his way."

"No one has seen us and nobody knows."

"You cannot be sure. At court everyone is suspect," Arbeas warned.

"I have faith we will be safe."

"What are your plans?" Arbeas asked.

"We do not know yet. But love gave me hope and revived my soul. We will plead my case in front of the emperor to set me free and to serve Rome. I think he may listen. I am convinced we shall be together, when I do not know, but that time will come."

As they parted Demetrius sensed relief at sharing his

feelings, yet doubt invaded his mind. Was it wise to speak to Arbeas? He dismissed his worry as foolish and unworthy. They have been friends since his enslavement. Arbeas had showed him how to survive slavery. They had shared their hopes, their dreams.

He closed his eyes and thought of Anastasia. For now she was his only in his thoughts. Soon she will be his for real. He fell into a pleasant sleep.

It was a day that started like any other day. Anastasia had risen early to finish summarizing a document on Christ's Resurrection which she intended to give to her uncle. There would be no Council meeting today and she planned to take the day relaxing.

According to rumors Valerius had returned and although she hadn't heard from him, her anxiety grew waiting for the unknown. Yet she dared to hope that while away, he had time to think about her refusal, and accepted her rejections with grace.

She walked to the dining hall where slaves were serving breakfast to the bishops and Council attendees. Usually they welcomed her politely and brought her honey cakes and fruit, but today was different. They met her with silence, their looks bordering on hostile.

"What is going on?" Anastasia asked a passing servant.

The young girl ignored her, avoiding eye contact and hurried to her destination. Anastasia turned to others, but they all passed her in silence, their heads to the ground, unwilling or afraid to speak.

Bewildered, she walked to a table and was ready to sit, when an elderly slave pulled her aside and out of sight. With eyes glaring he spoke. "Demetrius has escaped. He is a fugitive. Valerius will track him down and when he finds him he will torture him. There will be no mercy and he will die. It will reflect on the rest of us. Who knows what awaits us. You have caused all this."

"What are you saying?" she cried.

The man looked around and whispered, "I repeat, Demetrius escaped. Someone reported his meetings with you and he ran."

"Who reported him? Tell me."

"I do not know. There are spies everywhere."

"Where did he go?" she said her heart sinking.

"I don't know and wouldn't want to know."

"When did this happen? It couldn't have been long?

"Don't ask me questions. I spoke too much already. Do not repeat what I told you or I'm a dead man." He snuck away hiding his face as if shielding it from blows.

Anastasia turned pale. She was beside herself. Her thoughts were for Demetrius. She needed to find him, but where to look? She thought of his friend Arbeas and ran to the museum where she knew he'd be working. She had met Arbeas when Demetrius took her to see his sculptures.

So happy for him Demetrius was, his fellow Greek and friend, that after years of captivity he would be free, that whatever envy he felt for him was gone. She reached the museum out of breath and was almost inside when she heard voices. One of them she recognized immediately and shuddered. Slowly she tiptoed within earshot and hid behind a column.

"I paid you to keep me informed," Valerius said his voice low yet thundering with anger.

"Sir, I told you all I knew, as soon as I knew," Arbeas said.

"Not quick enough. He escaped right under your nose." Valerius voice intensified with anger.

"Sir, you were away and….."

"You had couriers at your disposal you miserable fool and should have sent me a message."

"Sir, I was waiting for more details."

"Details? When you knew they were meeting in secret? I pay you well for keeping me informed, too well."

Arbeas stood silent. He thought about his upcoming freedom. Was it all lost?

Valerius was pacing the floor. "I will deal with you later. Right now I want to know where Demetrius is and if anyone has helped him. If you fail me again you know what awaits you. Do you understand?"

"Yes, I understand." Lowering his head he thought of the mines. He would not last long.

Valerius left the museum fuming, his eyes glaring with

hate. Anastasia stood in shock, a statue, afraid to breathe, unable to think. Gradually anger and disgust soared within her as she looked at the man who betrayed his friend. What evil moved a man to sell his brother for thirty pieces of silver?

Gaining control she slipped away and walked towards the palace gardens. There she would organize her thoughts.

She had barely reached the gardens when a thought entered her mind. Constantia may be helpful. If not she might be sympathetic. With hope prompting her on she hurried towards Constantia's quarters. She had not been there before but knew she lived in the east wing of the palace. She wondered what would she say and how she would receive her, if at all.

Chapter 17

At the door of Constantia's quarters a maid servant let Anastasia inside not at all surprised. It was as if she was expected. She followed the maid through a long corridor with doors on both sides. At the end of the hall they came upon a large room furnished with recliners and sofas. A table with fruits and cakes stood in the middle. Candle chandeliers hung from the ceiling. The room's three walls were decorated with paintings of flowers and exotic plants, and the fourth side faced a garden surrounded with a wall which kept the garden private. In the corner of the room was a young slave girl playing the harp. The maid servant pointed to a chair and disappeared behind a heavy tapestry.

Anastasia sat squeezing her fingers as thoughts of betrayal passed through her mind. Why did Arbeas betray Demetrius? Was it the money or was it something else? What would compel a man to sell out his friend?

Light footsteps interrupted her thoughts, and raising her head she saw Constantia looking down at her. She rose, curtseyed and waited for Constantia to speak.

"Sit down my child," Constantia said sitting beside her. "I know why you are here. Yes, he is safe with me for the moment but he cannot stay long. I am already watched and under suspicion."

He was safe, was all she could think at the moment. When the moment passed and she regained her wits she turned to Constantia. "Your Highness, it is all my fault. I love him and put him at risk."

"It is both your faults," Constantia said somewhat angrily. "Demetrius knew the dangers. Love between a slave and free person is forbidden and severely punished. Those who harbor fugitives are considered traitors. You put us all at risk."

Anastasia hung her head and tears trickled down her cheeks.

Seeing her cry Constantia's face softened. She remembered her own love which ended in tragedy, and she felt pity for the young lovers. She lifted Anastasia's face and spoke.

"You were both foolish and chose a dangerous path. But your love is real and deep. Come with me, I will take you to him."

She led the way into a dark passage lit only by an occasional torch. At the end of the passage Constantia unlocked a door which led into an art gallery. They passed paintings and sculptures, some completed others half-finished, standing on tables and shelves of various sizes. Against one wall was a large shelf surrounded by fresh flowers and burning candles. On the shelf stood two large busts, one of a young boy and another of a man.

Pointing to them Constantia said, "my son and my husband, both murdered by my brother the emperor." She walked up to her husband's bust, said a few tender words and pressed her lips to his. Turning to her son, she stroked his face, kissed him on both cheeks and whispered, "my precious little boy. I will love you forever and will see you in heaven among the angels." A mother, a wife, grieving for her family, tears rolling down her cheeks.

After what seemed like a long time she pressed her hand against a panel on the side of the shelf. The shelf moved revealing a dark narrow tunnel. Bending low she crawled into it motioning Anastasia to follow. At the end of the tunnel was a small room. On a bed in a corner of the room sat Demetrius.

Anastasia stood in awe. Then with energy unknown to her before she rushed to him and fell into his open arms. As their lips met and the warmth of their bodies merged, all reality vanished, only their love prevailed.

They clung to each other unwilling to let go, when Constantia interrupted them and spoke to Anastasia. "You cannot stay long. It is dangerous for you to be here. By nightfall I will move Demetrius to my villa by the sea. He will be safe there until we know what action to take."

With tender words and tight embraces they finally said their farewells. Anastasia turned to Constantia and knelt in front of her. "Your Highness, I don't know how I will ever repay you. I am a stranger to you, a simple girl, and Demetrius is a slave. We are irrelevant, insignificant, you owe us nothing, and yet….."

"You are correct, I owe you nothing," Constantia interrupted. "I do this because I want to. My life has been laden with grief, yet I rejoice at making others happy. And if I can help, so I shall."

A servant approached and handed Constantia a package. She handed it to Demetrius who opened it. Inside were priest's vestments.

"You will disguise yourself as a Christian priest under my coat of arms. The guards are reluctant to arrest priests," she said to Demetrius. Turning to Anastasia she said, "you will have to leave now. Soon a carriage will take Demetrius away. There is much work to do."

Anastasia embraced Demetrius one last time and brought her lips to his. He held her close to his heart. "Whatever happens to me, I will always love you," he said his voice shaking with emotion. "If I die, my death would not be in vain, for you gave me happiness that comes only once."

Anastasia clung to him unable to let go. "I don't want to leave you. I cannot leave you." She began to cry.

"You must, only for a little while, my love. We will soon be together. I will think of a way. You must trust in me."

Anastasia let go. Would she ever see him again? Would he be a fugitive for the rest of his life, or would Valerius find him and end his life?

"Come my child," Constantia said. "We must think of a plan to save Demetrius."

She walked away holding on to Constantia, her knees caving in. She felt dizzy and the world spun around her. Slowly and gracefully she dropped to the floor like a wilting flower. Servants carried her to a room and laid her on a bed.

Images of Demetrius beaten and near death appeared before her. He was unconscious but they revived him and stretched him on a wheel. Screaming in agony he begged for death as he cried out her name. The cries became weaker, then stopped, and he was no more.

She rubbed her eyes to extinguish the image and saw Constantia bending over her. "Sleep my child and when you have rested we will form a plan."

Anastasia closed her eyes but did not sleep. A plan began to emerge to save Demetrius. It was mad, disgusting, and probably unattainable, but she had to try. She would have to sacrifice, and she gladly would, to save Demetrius.

She rose from bed thanking Constantia and left, dreading the repulsive road ahead she must take.

Chapter 18

Demetrius rose from bed and looked out of the window at the ocean below. Dark clouds were gathering over the horizon and signs of a storm became visible. Lightning over the water illuminated the waves, and thunder echoed in the distance. He did not like storms. They gave him a feeling of doom. Something would happen today he thought, what, he did not yet know.

He had been moved to Constantia's villa in the country with no apparent problems, where people of various backgrounds stayed as guests of the princess. To keep his identity secret, Demetrius masked himself as a Christian priest, studying the scriptures and Christian theology. He took his disguise seriously, going so far as to learn the rituals and customs of the faith. For a while he was safe but his future remained risky.

Today he washed his hands and face and put on his priestly garments, a white tunic to the ankles with a cord at the waist, a cloak with a hole in the center to admit the head, and a long narrow cloth that he placed around the neck. With a Bible in his hand he made his way towards the dining hall where slaves were preparing the first meal of the day. They acknowledged him with their bows, and seated him by a table where fruit, cakes, and honey cereals awaited him. Observing the slaves guilt overcame him. He was one of them, although they didn't know it. While he roamed freely in the villa and the coastline, they labored for their masters with no rewards.

Scripture passages on slavery in the letters of St. Peter and St. Paul troubled him. St. Peter wrote in his First Letter, Chapter 2, Verse 18. "*Slaves, be subject to your masters with all reverence, not only to those that are good and equitable but also to those that are perverse. For whenever anyone bears the pain of unjust suffering because of consciousness of God, that is grace.*"

And St. Paul wrote in his First Letter to Timothy, Chapter 6, Verse 1. "*Those who are under the yoke of slavery must regard their masters as worthy of full respect, so that the name of God and our teaching may not suffer abuse. Those whose masters are believers must not take advantage of them because they are brothers but must give them better service because those who will profit from their work are believers and are beloved.*"

But some passages gave him comfort as in St. Paul's Letter to the Colossians, Chapter 4, Verse 1. "*Masters, treat your slaves justly and fairly, realizing that you too have a Master in heaven.*"

Or when St. Paul tells the slaves to be obedient to their

masters in his Letter to the Ephesians, Chapter 6, Verse 5, he continues in the same paragraph urging the masters to stop bullying the slaves, Verse 9. *"Masters, act in the same way towards them, and stop bullying, knowing that both they and you have a Master in heaven and that with him there is no partiality."*

What gave Demetrius most comfort was St. Paul's passage in his Letter to the Galatians, Chapter 3, Verse 27. *"For all of you who were baptized into Christ have clothed yourselves with Christ. There is neither Jew nor Greek, there is neither slave nor free person, there is not male and female; for you are all one in Christ Jesus."*

Being Greek and having been raised in the Greek tradition that some people were slaves by nature, St. Paul's teaching that all were equal in the eyes of God brought new awareness to Demetrius. Becoming a slave himself he challenged slavery and saw its evil. He would have been a better man had he reached that conclusion when free.

All equal in the eyes of God but not equal in the eyes of people, so the holy men wrote. Demetrius wondered what would the Roman Empire be like if there were no slaves. Who would do the work? Would everything collapse or would free citizens pick up where slaves left off?

He knew the time was not yet ripe to shed slavery and many years away. Christianity, feeling the first waves of freedom, could not afford to challenge slavery. Chaos would follow. The pagans would rise, and if the emperor resisted they would depose him. Christianity already had changed the empire. Abolishing slavery would have to wait. Yet the Christian teachings of justice and kindness to slaves sowed seeds of freedom for all.

After finishing his breakfast Demetrius left the villa and walked towards the coastline. The weather was clearing and the storm was moving away. He loved the sound of the sea, and watch the sea gulls dip their long beaks into the water in search of fish. Alone and safe he could be himself and dream of Anastasia and their future together.

Constantia had sent word that she planned to move him to the Kingdom of Bosporus. The king, although friendly with the emperor was independent, and welcomed Greeks as teachers to his people. Would Anastasia be willing to leave her home and family, probably never to see them again? He wasn't sure, but deep in his heart he believed she would.

As he walked on the shore enjoying his thoughts tiny specks appeared on the horizon. As the specks enlarged the sound of galloping horses reached his ears, and Roman soldiers came into view. For a split second he hesitated, then realizing that he was finished, ran to the ocean. Deeper and deeper he sunk his feet in the ocean floor, until the bottom disappeared and the ocean covered his body. He held his breath until spasms of pain jolted his chest and he exhaled. Bubbles of air circled around him. Gasping for air, wanting to die yet fighting to live, he inhaled, and water entered his lungs. Freedom at last!

But death eluded him. Rough hands pulled him to the surface and threw him on the sand. He lay on his side coughing and gagging as water drained from his lungs letting him breathe. They stood him up and put chains on his hands and blindfold on his eyes. He felt a sudden jerk and a rope dragged him forward. Scornful laughter and brutal language surrounded him.

"Oh gods, let me die," he cried. "Oh Christian God, if you exist have mercy." He fell, his head hit a rock, and blood poured down his face. "I think I'm dying," he whispered then everything went black.

———※———

Demetrius opened his eyes but only darkness greeted him. He was lying on a wet floor, shivering from the cold trying to remember what happened. His hands were free and he reached for his eyes. The blindfold was gone. His head and body ached and scabs had formed on his wounds. He rose and felt the chains drag on his legs. The smell of human waste reached his nostrils. He sensed he was not alone. Taking a few steps he stopped. Something was blocking his path. Bending over he touched human flesh, cold and stiff. Shuddering, he walked back and sat against the wall, waiting, for what, he did not know.

How long he waited he wasn't sure, he may have even fallen asleep when the sound of keys broke the silence. The heavy iron door swung open. He heard the sound of footsteps, then someone waved a burning torch. Through the flames he saw a Roman soldier glaring down at him.

"So you're still alive, slave," the soldier said with disdain. "That's good because you're going on a trip. But before you leave there is someone who wants to see you." Saying that he laughed and wielded the torch in front of his face scorching his skin.

At that moment a man dressed in imperial uniform walked into his cell. Through the mist he recognized Valerius. His face showed the satisfaction that comes with capturing an enemy much despised. "So you tried to escape, is that right?" Valerius said. "That wasn't very smart, was it? You know that slaves should never try to escape, and if they do, well, they just better not." He paused, laughed with sarcasm, and walking to Demetrius kicked him in the stomach.

Demetrius doubled over and moaned. The pain was horrific. But in that instant something inside him stirred. He was aroused to let his voice be heard. Captivity had made him a shadow, but now the energy within him emerged, and the courage which had evaded him empowered him. He was a man weak in flesh but strong in will. Rising he stood eye to eye with Valerius. "You may break my body but never my spirit," he said.

Valerius retreated, taken aback. Then with affected authority said, "you are a slave and a slave you will die."

"I am in bondage but my soul is free and you will never own it."

The two men looked at each other, their eyes meeting in the battle of the words. Then Valerius called to his guard. "Get him ready for the quarry in Egypt. This is where he will go and where he will die."

He lifted his sword and placed it against Demetrius throat. "You are fortunate that killing slaves became illegal. But you will die in the quarry, anyway. A week or a month makes no difference. Your death warrant has already been signed." Saying that he kicked him again and left.

The guard approached Demetrius. "You will work in the hot sun, scraping granite from the rock until every fiber in your body will beg for death. But death will not come at your choosing. The guards will revive you to start the day again, until Valerius decides when you die."

In a strange way Demetrius felt free. The words did not disturb him. He will die a slave but his soul was freed. He had been liberated and his shackles were gone. Did the feeling of freedom come from the Bible? He recalled the Letter of St. Paul to the Galatians, Chapter 3, Verse 27, which had recently been on his mind. *"For all of you who were baptized into Christ have clothed yourselves with Christ. There is neither Jew nor Greek, there is neither slave nor free person, there is not male and female; for you are all one in Christ Jesus. And if you belong to Christ, then you are Abraham's descendant, heirs according to the promise.*

These words made him tremble, not from fear but from joy. He had not been baptized but his will to be, made him one with Christ. God did not have favorites.

He thought of Anastasia and wished she could share his joy. In his remaining days her love will sustain him. He will not see her again but will die a happy man.

Chapter 19

Unaware of Demetrius' capture Anastasia hoped for his continued safety. She knew Valerius was obsessed to find him, and he paid his spies well for information.

Today walking to the Council meeting, she spotted him from afar. He had recently returned from his mission and she was grateful that he left her alone. Seeing him in the distance she moved away so as not to be seen but it was too late. Valerius came towards her, smiling. "My lady, what a sweet surprise to see you," he said with genuine pleasure. "I have been busy but never too busy for you. I have not forgotten our last meeting and had intended to call on you."

Waiting for her reply which did not come he said, "have you thought about our last conversation, my proposal of marriage?"

She thought the question presumptuous yet she replied as before. "Sir, the answer is no. Do not make this hard on me. I do not take pleasure in refusing you."

"Do you still love Demetrius?"

How insolent she thought and hesitated to answer. Yet she needed to tell him the truth. "Yes, I love him, and always will," she said.

His face clouded and took on a malicious look. "Well, you might as well forget him. My guards captured him, and at this moment I am shipping him to a quarry in Egypt. He will hammer for granite in the hot sun until I decide when he dies. In reality his death will be a blessing to him but it will be at my command."

Anastasia cringed in shock. She recalled Demetrius' arms around her and her lips on his. She remembered his words to love her forever. Now she felt his suffering, toiling in the sun and writhing in pain. She will plead for his life.

"Sir, I ask you to set him free."

Valerius laughed. "Free? That is impossible. He was a fugitive and his punishment is just."

"Sir, if not his freedom, I beg for his life."

"Life? He has no life. If I'm disposed to let him die quickly, it will be a matter of weeks. The turnover of slaves is high in the quarries, few survive."

Was this the moment of truth she dreaded? Was this the sacrifice she promised to make? Keeping calm she spoke slowly almost in a whisper.

"Sir, I will marry you if you save his life." She closed her eyes not to see his face.

Valerius laughed, taken aback, unable to hide his

amusement. "So, you wish to negotiate. You would marry me to save your lover. I would not have foreseen this. You are amazing."

"Sir, I will make you a good wife."

"I believe you would. But I hesitate to accept the terms. I want you freely without conditions."

"If you grant me this wish I will never ask for anything again."

"It's very noble of you."

"Then do as I ask," she pleaded.

What seemed like eternity Velerius finally spoke. "I will grant your wish and not send him to the quarries on two conditions. That you never see Demetrius again, and will not ask questions about him. He will remain my slave, and where I send him you will not know. His education will be useful for some of the projects that I have in mind."

A sense of relief overcame her. In an odd way she felt sympathy for Valerius, a bitter and unhappy man, getting his way through force and intimidation. Yet with the relief doubt entered her mind. Was his word good? She wasn't sure but she had no choice.

"I will abide by your conditions," she said.

"It's settled then. I will inform the emperor of our up-coming marriage, and you may prepare for your wedding." His face softened and for a moment a spark of tenderness appeared. "I will be a good husband and make you happy. You will not want for anything. You may not believe me, but I truly love you," he said reaching for her hand and kissing it.

She let him kiss it.

As they parted Anastasia knew that her life would change forever.

Valerius walked to his quarters. There, taking aside one of his guards, his voice cold, his words ruthless, he said, "give Demetrius double duty at the quarry, minimum of food and water, and no shelter from the sun. He will not survive long. I want him dead the sooner the better. Tell no one of this or you will face the consequences."

The guard saluted and began to plan Demetrius' demise. Valerius pleased at the outcome turned his attention to the emperor's business.

Chapter 20

Anastasia began to prepare for her wedding with a heavy heart. She dreaded her future as Valerius' wife, and wondered if she could even begin to like him. But he promised to save Demetrius' life and this was what mattered. She would make the best of her marriage and find peace knowing that he was safe. Maybe Valerius would free him later and he would start a new life, even find happiness with a wife. And maybe in time she would look kindly at Valerius and be grateful to him for what he had done. She would never love him, that she knew, but knowing that Demetrius was safe was worth her sacrifice.

Valerius had sent her flowers soon after their meeting, and a pearl necklace which he asked her to wear at their wedding. It was his mother's he said in the note, and his grandmother's before that, and he hoped in time it would pass to their daughter. She resented the flowers and the necklace, they reminded her of what awaited her, but felt compelled to accept them.

As her mind wandered in many directions, questions

frequently arose to which she had no answers. Was she willing to live a lie for the rest of her life? The lie that she did not love Valerius. In her heart she knew her plan was dishonest, and it lay heavy on her conscience. Could she be Valerius' wife and love Demetrius instead? Could she bear to have his arms around her? The thought repulsed her, and yet this was what loomed ahead. Was Demetrius worth her sacrifice? Did he love her enough for what she was doing? There were moments of doubt. At times she wanted to renege on her marriage and be free again, but the image of Demetrius in a quarry stopped her.

She tried to justify the falsehood of her marriage with a passage from the Gospel of John, Chapter 15, Verse 13. *"No one has greater love than this, to lay down one's life for one's friends."*

Wasn't that what she was doing? Giving her life for a friend? Not in the physical sense, but emotionally, giving up her happiness which was her life, without which she would be emotionally dead. She thought about it and began to doubt her reasoning. Sacrificing happiness no matter how deep is not a physical death. Demetrius was her friend, but also the man she loved romantically, different from what Jesus had in mind.

Another thought chiseled at her mind. She had not confided in her uncle. She dreaded to tell him yet realized he needed to know. She decided to be forthright.

Next day she took her uncle aside, and finding a bench spoke quickly to get it off her chest. "I have decided to marry Velerius. He loves me and I will make him a good wife."

Expecting to see him shocked, the bishop's face took on a troubled look. "I cannot say that I am happy, in fact I am worried." He paused for a minute then chose his words carefully. "I do not know why you are doing it. It's not in your nature to go against your heart. You do not love him and told me so yourself." His face became sad and a tear trickled down his one eye. "Why the marriage?" he asked.

Determined to tell all, Anastasia opened her heart and told her uncle about Demetrius, their love for each other, their secret meetings, and Arbeas' betrayal. In the end she told of Demetrius' escape and his capture. She began to cry, overcome by emotion. Finally she answered what the bishop wanted to know.

"Uncle, I made a pact with Valerius. He is obsessed with me and wants me for his wife. He promised to spare Demetrius' life and in return I would marry him." When she finished speaking she was at the point of collapse.

Shocked at what he heard the bishop rose in alarm. "My child, for a Roman woman to love a slave is against the law. God only knows what would happen if the emperor knew. You must forget Demetrius and never talk about it. And cancel the wedding. Your reason for marriage is wrong, an insult to holy matrimony. It is in bad faith and not God's way. Be true to God and yourself."

"He is a slave but I love him and cannot forget him. There's no other way to save him. The quarry was his death and that I could not bear. I will not see him but knowing that he is alive will give me peace. And maybe one day Valerius will set him free."

"My child think what you are doing. You will live a lie for the rest of your life and live to regret it. Nothing good can come of this, only misery." He paused to calm down and when he resumed his tone was soft. "My child, the Council will soon be over and we will go home. We've been away too long. You will be back with your friends and all will pass with time."

"I will always love Demetrius. And to let him live I must marry Valerius. I will suffer more by letting him die than by marrying Valerius."

The bishop realized he lost. "Do as you wish. I will pray for you and leave all to God." He recalled Anastasia's mother forceful stand when she insisted on marrying a pagan. But circumstances were different. They were both free.

He kissed his niece and walked away shaking his head. Oh God, give her strength and wisdom, he prayed.

Chapter 21

Relieved at sharing her secret yet troubled by her uncle's words, Anastasia's emotions were in turmoil. She was alone in her decision. Will anyone understand? She longed for her mother whom she hardly remembered. She needed her now, to guide and protect her, to bring her to her breast and wipe away her tears. But her mother was dead, a Christian martyr dying for her faith. Yet what about the child that she left behind, an orphan, with both parents dead? Was she obliged to live for her child? For the first time that she could remember Anastasia felt deprived.

Sitting in the garden and listening to the birds chip, she wondered what she would do if she had to choose between her child and her faith? Surely such choices did not apply to mothers. Mothers were exempt from making them. A mother's love was unconditional. Choice was never an option. But fathers were different. There was Abraham in the Bible.

She covered her face with her hands and unleashed

her emotions. "Oh mother, I need you now. Why did you abandon me? Did you not love me when you chose to die for your faith?"

At that moment she felt a hand on her shoulder, and turning around saw Constantia.

Jumping up and curtseying she blurted out, "Your Highness, please forgive me. I did not see you coming."

"Sit down Anastasia," Constantia said helping the girl back to her seat. "Do not waste your tears for things you cannot change. Your mother did what she thought was right, what her conscience told her, and you must accept it and not judge her. You do not know what was in her heart." She embraced the crying girl and taking out a kerchief wiped her tears. "If you want a mother's comfort I will be your mother. I have no one to care for since I lost my child. My son will always remain in my heart, but you can be my daughter that I never had."

"Your Highness, you are too good to me. In your sorrow you found it in your heart to care about me. Yes, be my mother and I will cherish it always." She knelt before Constantia and kissed her hand.

"Enough of this," Constantia said helping her rise. "I know your distress and I'm here to comfort you. Demetrius' capture was unforeseen. Valerius' spies have been at work. There was nothing I could have done to prevent it. I dread to say it, but his days are numbered. You must now move forward with your life, and I will help you recover."

"But Demetrius will live! He is saved!" Anastasia cried

with excitement, her emotions at peak. " I agreed to marry Valerius and in return he promised to save his life. True, my marriage is unusual, and I do not love him, but knowing that Demetrius is safe I can live with my future. I will be a good wife and he promised to be a good husband."

Constantia listened patiently and when Anastasia finished she spoke. Her tone was firm but kind. "Marrying one man and loving another is a formula for misery. It's not fair to you nor to Demetrius, not even to Valerius. How do you think Demetrius would feel knowing you sold yourself for his sake? He would prefer death. In time you will resent your husband, even hate him. I dread to predict what may happen."

"Valerius loves me and will be good to me," Anastasia said trying to be reassuring.

"Valerius may love you but it's not the love of a husband for his wife. I know Valerius. His love is possessive and controlling. He is obsessed with you. I have seen his eyes follow you, and I do not like what they say. Nothing good will come of it."

"There must be some good in him," Anastasia said.

"If there is I do not see it. He is ambitious and ruthless, you have seen that yourself. He will kill if necessary and will lie about it." She stopped and pondered for a moment. "I am sure he has murdered innocent people and caused havoc among the troops, but I have no proof. Deep in my heart I fear for the emperor's safety. I dare not say what is on my mind."

E.D.S. SMITH

Anastasia looked surprised. "The emperor trusts Valerius. He has many faults but his loyalty is beyond reproach."

"The emperor is surrounded by sycophants who flatter him and tell him what he wants to hear. Valerius is the best of them all. He will say anything to please the emperor and raise his standing, and he knows how to do it. But his motives are treacherous. I warn you my daughter, take heed."

"I have to follow the only path I have to save Demetrius," Anastasia said.

The two women parted in friendship as well as sorrow. When Constantia kissed her, she said, "if you need me I will come. My senses tell me it will be soon. I fear danger lurking by your side."

Anastasia felt a chill. Constantia's doubts of Valerius' loyalty distressed her. She recalled the deaths of the five unarmed men on their way to Thessalonica, who Valerius said were pagans on a mission to kill Christians. Nothing was proven or reported at court. Did Valerius cover up the killings? Were the soldiers with him his accomplices? And the infighting of Christians at the banquet in Constantinople? Her uncle had doubted that Christians were fighting. He feared it was staged, a conspiracy to weaken the empire. Thoughts of treason raced through her mind. Was Valerius a traitor? Impossible. She dismissed the thoughts and tried to forget them, but they lingered on.

Chapter 22

Several days passed and Anastasia absorbed herself in the Council's business. Reluctantly she prepared for her wedding which was to take place in the palace chapel. More presents arrived which she stacked in her room, loath to look at them. They reminded her of her future, a future that she dreaded more each day. She felt wretched, living a lie, betraying everyone and most of all herself. Her only comfort was that she was saving Demetrius.

Today she felt especially bitter. She needed to think, to re-evaluate her plans, to find peace with what she was doing or withdraw. There was still time, but then what about Demetrius? No, she must follow her course for the sake of Demetrius.

She took a stroll along the beach until she came to the docks where ships sailed to and from all parts of the empire. The weather had been stormy, the sea rough, delaying the sail. From a distance she saw a large ship loading slaves to Egypt. The men were bound by chains and chained to each other with no chance of escape.

A sad feeling came upon her again. "Poor fellows," she said looking at the pitiful men, knowing their lives at the mines would be short and brutal. At this moment she felt justified in marrying Valerius. She had saved Demetrius' life.

Coming closer to the docks she spotted women slaves loading baskets of bread and buckets of water on board. They were silent, their heads bowed, their old faces depicting despair, reflecting the human injustice of which they were victims. When they were young and pretty, Romans had used them to satisfy their lust, now in their old age, they ended their lives feeding other slaves. The scene again stirred her conscience on slavery. When will it end?

She was about to go back not wanting to look at the misery when one slave caught her eye. He was standing on the dock waiting to board and something about him was different. He had a beard which hid most of his face, but the way he stood seemed familiar. He was erect and held his head high. Anastasia became unnerved. He reminded her of someone. She wanted to leave yet something pulled her towards him.

She came close to him, almost within reach. His head was turned and he didn't see her. She tried to get his attention but didn't know how. The guards with whips struck anyone who spoke. She thought for a moment then acted. Falling down to the ground she cried out in pain and held her ankle. The slave turned around and their eyes met. It was Demetrius.

He looked down at her bewildered. For a moment he

said nothing, then recognizing her he cried out, "I will love you forever even when I die." He had barely uttered the words when a guard swung his whip and struck him with full force. He stumbled but did not fall. Another blow followed and another and another, until he dropped to the ground. Anastasia watched as slaves dragged his bloody body to the bowels of the ship.

Rage, grief, and a sense of betrayal surged within her. She began to stumble. Helpful hands picked her up and placed her in a carriage that took her to the palace. "A monster, sub-human, an evil man," she kept repeating as tears rolled down her cheeks.

They took her to her quarters where she lay down in bed, her spirit crushed but not defeated. Her thoughts turned to saving Demetrius. But how? Overtaken with exhaustion she fell into an unsettled sleep.

———•((◊))•———

It was dark when she awoke. The stars were flickering in the sky, and the full moon was illuminating the room. In spite of her troubled sleep she felt rested and her mind was clear. She knew the first thing she had to do.

She knelt by a statuette of the Virgin and prayed. She realized her plan to marry Valerius was wrong. It was a lie, a betrayal of God and herself. Her uncle and Constantia had warned her but she took no heed. God had saved her and she had time to undo it. She would find a way to save Demetrius, and that would begin with the truth.

She waited for dawn preparing and rehearsing her speech, letting her reason guide her. With the first sign of daybreak she was ready, and walked to Valerius' quarters asking to see him.

"Of course, my lady," the slave said escorting her to a parlor, a smile on his face because she was well liked by his staff.

After a few minutes she heard familiar footsteps. She stood silent and still, as a statue cemented to the floor, gathering her courage.

"My lady, what a pleasure to see you," Valerius said smiling, taking her hand and bending to kiss it.

She pulled away.

He frowned but said nothing.

Looking into his cold eyes and hating him, she abandoned the speech she had memorized and spoke from her heart. Her voice was shaky yet inside she felt brave and composed. "You lied and betrayed me. I saw Demetrius on a ship waiting to sail to the mines. You promised to keep him safe."

Taken aback he looked confused. Trying to collect his thoughts he finally said, "circumstances changed. I was forced to alter my course of action"

"What circumstances?"

He thought again then said, "there is a shortage of slaves in the mines and we need every one of them."

"I do not believe you. You never intended to keep your promise," she shouted her poise disappearing. "I don't trust you anymore. I'm cancelling the wedding."

His lips tightened, his eyes narrowed. His look was icy. He came to Anastasia and gripped her arm. "You are my betrothed, my intended. You will not change your mind and dishonor me."

"You have dishonored yourself. As for me it is never too late to right a wrong. I should have never consented to marry you. It was wrong from the beginning. I will never marry you. You do not know me. I would rather die than become your wife."

"Take heed of your words. If I cannot have you, no-body will."

"What do you mean?" she said her face turning pale.

"It means you will never belong to anyone else."

"What will you do? Kill me if I marry another?" She mocked him but felt a chill inside and wished she hadn't said it.

A minute of silence and then Valerius spoke. "I am going away on the emperor's business for a few weeks. I expect you to wed me when I return." His face took on a kindly look and he said, "Anastasia, we've had a bad start today. Let us start the day again. I do want to please you, you know."

"I despise you. There is nothing more to say. I never want to see you. Get out of my life."

She turned to go but he blocked her way. "Please, listen

to me. I love you and always will. We'll have a good life together. You will have the freedom to do what you want. I promise you."

"Step aside and never bother me again. I love another."

He grimaced in anger. "With the first sign of good weather the slave ship will sail to Egypt and Demetrius will be on it. He will die and you will never see him again. So get him out of your mind. When I return we shall marry." He stepped aside and let her pass.

Exhausted and frightened she ran to her quarters and collapsed on the bed. The few minutes with Valerius seemed like hours of horror. She was drained of energy and sapped of all strength. She would not go to the Council today. She needed to recuperate and think what to do. Saving Demetrius was now her only thought. But the time was short.

Chapter 23

The weather had been stormy for which Anastasia was grateful. The seas were rough preventing the slave ship from sailing, and that meant she had a little more time to save Demetrius. Her reasoning told her that it was hopeless. How can a man be rescued that is chained and guarded day and night? And yet against all odds she did not give up hope. She prayed for help, for a miracle. She was one girl against an empire, but there were other means besides force of winning a battle. She must think of a plan and one began to emerge.

She was deliberating when a knock on the door interrupted her thoughts. Who would come to see her at this time? Somewhat cautiously she cracked open the door and peeked. On the other side of the door stood Arbeas.

Stunned, yet able to react she pushed the door back, but Arbeas forced his hand and barred it from closing.

"Go away, you traitor," she said.

"My lady, please give me a minute. My conscience will not let me sleep and I must redeem myself."

"Redeem? You are beyond redemption. Some acts are unforgivable. You sold your friend for thirty pieces of silver. I was there and heard everything. You are a Judas."

"I may have done what Judas did, but I am no Judas. I want to make amends. I want Demetrius to live."

"Live? Oh yes, he will live a week or two, maybe even a month, but he is doomed to die."

"I came to help in any way I can. There is still time to save him."

"I do not believe you. Why are you really here?"

"My lady, believe me. I am here to help save him and more. I want you to forgive me for what I did. Most of all I want Demetrius to say the word. My life is wretched. The guilt chisels at my soul."

Anastasia looked at Arbeas and something inside her said he was sincere. She believed him. She saw a tortured man, beaten and stripped of dignity. His eyes were listless, his expression hopeless, his face marked with deep furrows. His hair disheveled, his tunic stained, he looked like a beggar in the slums of Rome.

"Are you yet a free man?" she asked

"No, I am still a slave. Valerius had my mistress delay my freedom. She is away and for the present Constantia is my mistress. She knows of my remorse and has forgiven me. However, I am not at liberty to move around."

Anastasia thought for a moment. "You came here at a grave risk to your future, did you not?"

"I did with no regrets. Freedom would mean nothing

unless I can sleep at night."

He was still behind the door so Anastasia let him in.

"How do you propose to save Demetrius?" she asked. "He is chained and guarded."

"We have our minds to form a plan."

Was he the miracle she was praying for? Was he sent to help rescue Demetrius? Her mind was at work and a plan was evolving. It was based on trickery. Battles have been won by deception.

"I'm thinking of the story of the Trojan horse, and how the Greeks tricked the Trojans to enter the city of Troy," she said. "They built a wooden horse and placed few soldiers inside. The Trojans thinking it was a trophy of war pulled it into the city. At night, the soldiers inside the horse came out, and opened the city gates to let the rest of the army in. The Greeks won the battle and ended the war." She paused for a moment then added, "I'm thinking of tricking the guards."

"My lady, I think we can do it."

Anastasia's mind raced. At this very moment she knew there was a chance. Somehow they must deceive the guards, but how? She had no answer yet. She closed her eyes and thought. After a while she said, "I have a plan and we will need Constantia's help. It's dangerous and risky and may not succeed, but there is a chance."

"I'm listening."

She shared her plan and finished by saying, "The princess must help us. Without her nothing can be done."

"Once we rescue Demetrius my friends can smuggle him out of Nicaea and into freedom," Arbeas said.

"Then it's settled. Meet me in the morning by the princess' quarters. I shall ask for her help," Anastasia said.

With that they parted to meet early next day.

As Anastasia prepared for bed she felt hopeful. She tossed in bed thinking and planning, confident the plan might work. She fell asleep amidst hope and fear, but mostly hope.

Chapter 24

Next morning as soon as the sun rose Anastasia dressed and made her way to Constantia's quarters. From afar she saw Arbeas waiting for her.

They knocked on the door and a slave girl admitted them. They followed her through the long hall until they came to the reception area that Anastasia remembered. Fruits and cakes awaited them, and a young slave girl was playing the harp. She smiled at Anastasia, a warm and friendly smile.

Few minutes later Constantia walked in. She was dressed in a casual robe without adornments or jewelry. Her head was bare, the hair shoulder length without curls, and her face clear without paint. Anastasia thought how young she looked without her finery and jewels. Constantia smiled faintly, asked them to sit, then inquired about their business.

Anastasia unable to hold back began to speak. Her speech was fast and passionate, but she made her point and explained the plan. "I beg Your Highness to consider the plan," she concluded.

Constantia listened politely and with compassion for the young girl's hopes of rescuing her lover. When Anastasia finished, Constantia waited a moment then looked straight at Anastasia. She could not help but be amused.

"You want to disguise yourself as me, and together with Arbeas who will act as a court official, order the captain to release Demetrius so he can be questioned on a theft of my jewelry? Is that right?"

"Yes, Your Highness," Anastasia replied meekly.

"And what proof will you have to obtain his release?"

"A document from you stating that your precious pendant is missing, and that you suspect Demetrius of stealing."

Constantia smiled. "And then what?"

Arbeas broke into the conversation and spoke with excitement. "I will smuggle him out of Nicaea, north across the sea to the Kingdom of Bosporus, where Rome has no jurisdiction and where he can start a new life. I intend to go with him and take my sweetheart. I have saved enough money to make the trip and pay off the guards on the way. Anastasia of course may come too."

When he had finished speaking silence ensued. Anastasia fidgeted, her heart racing, her hopes dwindling the longer the silence remained.

Constantia walked to a chair and seated herself by a table asking the others to sit beside her. Still amused she tried to hide it. She called to the slave girl to bring break-fast, and the three of them ate cereal with honey, dates and fruit, and washed it down with diluted wine. Anastasia could hardly control herself, eating little and saying noth-ing, realizing she must remain silent until Constantia spoke.

When everyone had finished and the table had been cleared, Constantia turned to the two of them. "Your plan is a fantasy, an illusion. It's sincere but naïve and unwork-able. It's a dream of lovers reaching for the stars." She paused for a moment then looking at Anastasia said, "you would never pass disguised as me. I am well known not only by my looks but by the way I speak, walk, and by my servants who accompany me. Besides, I do not wish to have you caught for impersonating a member of the royal family. It is against the law and the consequences would be grave. You would be disgraced and sent back to Rome and Arbeas would end up in the mines."

Anastasia's heart sank. She had hoped against hope that Constantia would help, and now all seemed lost.

"But I will help you," Constantia broke the silence. "I will approach the captain myself and demand Demetrius' release. What excuse if any I will use, I will share with you later. I still have influence at the palace and the captain will not doubt me." She turned to Arbeas. "When I speak with the captain you will come with me. I know you have repented for betraying Demetrius and I trust you. Since you are still a slave loaned to the palace by your mistress and under my jurisdiction, your presence by my side will not be questioned."

"Your Highness, if the plot is revealed you will suffer the consequences. We wanted to spare you this and take on the plot ourselves. Even though you are the emperor's sister, Valerius may want to harm you," Arbeas said.

"He cannot harm me more than I am already. I am not afraid of him. His evil will catch up with him. God will judge him. But at this moment he is away on my brother's business and will not take action until he returns. Leave it to me to take care of the matter. I will do what I have to, and will handle my brother when the time arrives."

"Your Highness, why are you doing this?" Anastasia asked tearfully.

"I told you Anastasia, I am an empty shell, there is nothing within me. I am dead inside and do not care what happens to me. But I want young lovers to live and love. Let's not dwell on this. There is little time and we must hurry. The weather is clearing and the ship may soon sail. We must act fast."

What shall you have us do, Your Highness?" Arbeas said.

"Wait for my word. I will contact you when I'm ready. Be available to act as soon as you hear from me." Turning to Anastasia she said, "it is up to you whether you go or not, but do not delay their escape. They will have to move fast."

With that they parted. Anastasia went to her room

and Arbeas to the slave quarters to wait. As she contemplated the change of plans, Anastasia's thoughts were on Constantia. What made a person be charitable to others after so much suffering? There was no bitterness in Constantia's heart, no wish for revenge. Instead, compassion and willingness to help others guided her actions. She said she was hollow inside, but Anastasia disagreed. Something inside her remained, something good and noble.

As she pondered the plan, Anastasia wondered if they would succeed in freeing Demetrius, or was it a dream against the Roman machine. Only time would tell, yet she must have hope.

Chapter 25

It was dark and cold in the bowel of the ship as Demetrius and other slaves waited for the ship to sail. Several days had passed since Valerius' guards captured, beat, and tortured him, and put him on the ship to Egypt's mines. Now chained and unable to move if only to change positions, he welcomed the prospect of dying under the sun, his hands and feet free mining the granite. Death was a luxury for which he was ready and to which he aspired, and hoped to gain soon. Even the guards' whips did not bother him. Having seen Anastasia even for a moment, and telling her he loved her was worth a thousand lashes. His joy will stay with him until his last hour.

He looked around him and in the dimness of the cabin saw fellow slaves, some Greek, some from Gaul, and others from Syria, Spain, and as far away as Britain, identified by the language they spoke. Even though forbidden to speak, they managed a few words with each other. On one side of him sat a slave from Britain who had hit his master when he had assaulted his slave wife. The wife begged for mercy for her husband but to no avail. She remained at his master's house and he was sentenced to the mines forever. "And the master was a Christian too," the slave told Demetrius in broken Greek. "Didn't Christ teach mercy and forgiveness?"

On the other side was an old man whose withered body and gaunt face projected a pitiful sight. He was mumbling something under his breath in a language which Demetrius did not understand. Surprisingly, the guards let him mumble and laughed at him when they passed by him. Demetrius soon understood why. The man was not in his right mind. He was muttering nonsense, oblivious to his surrounding, his gaze far away, his expression empty. Demetrius wondered why he was there. What could an old feeble man have done to deserve this punishment? He looked educated and may have lost his mind when taken slave. Many have suffered shock when taken into captivity, and unable to adjust, lost touch with reality. He felt compassion and kinship for the man. He could have been his father.

He watched the others and pondered how they were captured, and how long they have been slaves. What were their lives before slavery, or were they born into it? What had they done to be sent to the mines, a place from which nobody returned? A feeling of comradeship came over him. He will share their fate, his life will entwine with theirs, they will help each other until one by one each falls down to the ground and dies. Knowing he was not alone gave him peace and the ability to accept his fate.

They had just finished a meager meal of grain and water when suddenly voices were heard above. One was a female and the other male which Demetrius recognized as that of the captain. Listening attentively, Demetrius heard the discussion.

"I want this slave released to my custody," the female's voice was subdued which he could not identify.

"My orders were that he sail to Egypt to work in the mines," the captain said.

"He had been loaned to me and is under my jurisdiction, and so remains until the loan is revoked. Here is the document confirming the loan and terms of the loan. I take full responsibility for him," the female said.

The captain glanced at the document but did not read it. Seeing the official stamp, and now recognizing the woman in front of him, he bowed and said, "at your command." He called to a guard and gave an order.

The hatch to the cabin opened and a guard called, "Demetrius the Greek, identify yourself."

Hearing his name called, terror struck Demetrius.

When there was no answer the captain cried out again. "Speak up Demetrius the Greek. I'll find you and when I do I will ....."

"I am Demetrius, the Greek," he called out timidly.

The guard stepped down into the cabin and came to him. Taking the key from his waist he unlocked the iron shackles from his hands and feet, ordered him to rise, and kicked him up the stairs onto the deck. "Lucky you. But you'll be back," he said with sarcasm. He laughed and kicked him again.

Shading his eyes from the light, Demetrius breathed for the first time in days the fresh air denied him before. The air was invigorating and he took deep breaths enjoying the moment.

Slowly and deliberately he turned his eyes to the two people standing before him. He blinked again and again, until the vision before him turned to reality. Before him stood Constantia and Arbeas.

Without speaking Arbeas grabbed Demetrius by the arm and with Constantia by his side led him to a waiting carriage. Demetrius tried to push him away but Arbeas whispered, "Do not fight me. I have much to explain."

There was no time to talk. With speed they rode to Constantia's villa. Upon arrival the three hurried to an inner room and knocked on the door. Anastasia opened it.

Every muscle in her body tightened. She could not speak, she could not think. She stood like a statue, absorbing the moment, waiting to see if he was real. Yes, he was real, standing beside her, his body beaten yet alive. The unbelievable had happened. Demetrius and she were united.

She took a few steps towards him and wavered. He caught her in his arms and pressed her to his heart. She nestled in his embrace and snuggled to him. Closing her eyes she brought her lips to his, and melted in his arms. They did not speak. They didn't have to. It would break the spell. Clinging to each other the world did not exist, only their love was real.

"The time is short," Constantia said breaking the spell. She turned to Demetrius. "You must be on your way. Arbeas arranged for a boat to take you north across the sea to the Kingdom of Bosporus. It is outside Roman jurisdiction. The people are pagan, but they welcome Christians who have established a small community there. Besides, they value Greek and Roman expertise so you will be doubly welcome. You will not be hunted there."

"Her Highness is right. We had better start moving," Arbeas said, fidgeting and looking at Demetrius with unease. "My fiancé is waiting by the boat."

Demetrius looked at Arbeas shaking his head. "You have betrayed me and now expect me to trust you? It is not possible. Even if your intentions were honorable I would not accept your help. I will make my own escape."

"If you only knew my guilt you would pity me," Arbeas pleaded. "I will make it up to you in a thousand ways. Desire for freedom overshadowed my sense of decency and loyalty. It wasn't only the money, although that was part of it, but the obsession to be free at any cost and soon. Valerius promised me instant freedom and I fell for it. I wish it had never happened. I ask you to forgive me and put the past behind you."

"Forgive you? Never. Look at my scars from the beatings. Look at my wounds from the chains. These can never be removed."

He had barely finished speaking when he thought of the wife who begged for mercy for her husband who had struck his master. The master was unforgiving. Was he playing the master? Maybe. Yet his bitterness lingered and would not give him peace.

"You must go with Arbeas and put your feelings aside," Anastasia said gently embracing Demetrius. "Her Highness has taken great risks to free you. You would be ungrateful if you didn't go. Give up your anger and resentment and try to forgive. Besides," she cradled his face in her hands, "it was at my pleading that she agreed to free you. I love you and want you to live. Do it for me."

"And what is to become of us?" Demetrius asked.

"Only God knows," Anastasia said tearfully.

Constantia who stood in the background now stepped forward and faced Demetrius. "You must go and trust Arbeas to help you. He has repented for what he did. If you want to live there is no other way. It's now or never."

For a moment Demetrius hesitated then turned to Arbeas. "I will go with you but I cannot forgive you."

"I understand," Arbeas said. "Perhaps with time.....," his voice trailed. Then with a sorrowful look he said, "we leave immediately for the northern coast where my fiancé awaits. I have a carriage waiting to take us there." He handed Demetrius a package tied with a string. "Take these and put them on. They will protect your identity."

Demetrius opened the package and unraveled a monk's robe.

"Hurry," Arbeas said. "You will travel as a missionary, and I and my fiancé will be your assistants. We know enough about the Christian faith to pass." With that he began to help Demetrius dress, and when he finished threw a cloak over himself, the kind that many Christians wore.

It was time to part. Demetrius looked at Anastasia and said, "Will you come with me?"

"I will join you, but not now. When, I do not know." Before she finished speaking she burst into tears.

Shaken at seeing her cry Demetrius took her in his arms one final time. "My sweet wife to be, I will write you and wait for you to join me. Our letters will speak of our love until the day we meet again."

They kissed for the last time, a long and passionate kiss, until Arbeas came between them and took Demetrius away. Anastasia watched as they boarded the coach and sped away. She waved until the coach was out of sight.

That night lying in bed she struggled with her thoughts. Will she see him again, or will the separation dim the fire in both their hearts, leaving a faint memory of what might have been. And when the time came for her to go, would she be willing to leave her home and uncle and go into the unknown? Would her love be enough to take that step? Time will tell. Feeling anxious and very tired she fell into an uneasy sleep.

Chapter 26

Days passed and Valerius hadn't returned. Happy at not having to face him Anastasia kept busy with the Council and thoughts of Demetrius. But thinking of Demetrius brought their future to the forefront, and with it her marriage to Valerius. Would she dare to approach the emperor, and in the spirit of Christian teachings ask him to release her from a marriage to which she was opposed. After all, didn't Christianity forbid marriage unless both parties willingly consented? And could she press him further to forgive Demetrius and set him free? Was she dreaming the impossible, and yet, wouldn't that be the Christian thing to do?

She decided to see the emperor but each time she tried she failed. Her attempts to see Constantia were also futile. She learned that she was away at her country villa with no definite date of return. Anastasia was at a loss.

She sensed that something secretive was happening at the court. People were congregating in small groups and whispering among themselves. Even the bishops looked anxious, although the proceedings of the Council continued at a normal pace. Eventually the tension turned to foreboding that something bad will happen, or already has. Anastasia approached her friends as well as her uncle, yet nobody had an answer. All she could gain from her questions was that in some way it involved the emperor.

It was one of those days when everything was going according to schedule that tragic news reached the court. The Council had adjourned early so the bishops could enjoy the ocean breeze, and a meal of Egyptian delicacies prepared by Egyptians cooks. The mood was subdued but relaxed, as the bishops tasted the antelope meat served with dates and peaches, along with gazelles tenderloins served with grapes and watermelon. Waiters circulated among the bishops pouring wine and beer.

While they were eating a servant arrived out of breath, and murmured something into the presiding bishop's ear. The bishop turned pale, wiped his brow and rose to address the group.

"My fellow bishops. The court has confirmed that the emperor's oldest son Crispus, commander of the Roman legions in Gaul has been killed. He was very popular with the army and the citizens at large. Details are vague and the manner of his death unknown. No announcement of his death will be made by the emperor."

He paused and with a strained face added, "no more information will be forthcoming and any attempts to explain his death will be suppressed, and those responsible for speaking will be punished. The emperor has ordered that his son's name never be mentioned again."

The bishops listened in silence with shock and disbelief on their faces. When the initial blow had passed, they began whispering among themselves, sharing their comments and sorrow, and the secretive circumstances of his death. Although they had never met Crispus, his reputation as an honorable man, a brave soldier, and brilliant commander was known to all. He was loved and respected by all Romans, and everyone expected that one day he would succeed his father.

The presiding bishop clapped his hands to gain the bishops attention. "I advise you, I urge you my fellow bishops, not to speak to the emperor about it. We shall pray for the young soldier, his widow, and baby son who lost a husband and a father."

The bishops rose and the presiding bishop led them in prayer. When they finished praying they continued their meal, but the mood was somber. They began to speculate on what happened. Where, how, and why was he killed were the questions they asked but could not answer. Was he in a battle and killed by an enemy? Or was he murdered by one of his own? Was it a dagger or poison? Perhaps a captive got loose and stabbed him in his sleep. Impossible. The prisoners were chained and guarded with no means of escape. Was it a mutiny that ended in murder? Unlikely, considering the troops' devotion to Crispus. And even if there was mutiny, wouldn't the emperor have sent troops to defend his son? Perhaps an accident took his life? Did he fall off the horse or drown in the river? Highly improbable. The man was an athlete and an excellent equestrian. And why did secrecy surround his death, and his name forbidden to be spoken? As the emperor's son and heir to the empire, shouldn't he be given a funeral befitting royalty, laid in a golden coffin, and entombed in a place of honor? The lack of information and the strange way in which his death was handled, created uncertainty and tension amongst the bishops and the palace at large.

The bishops finished their meal, and after exhausting all explanations, scattered to their quarters, confused, sad, and eager for reliable news.

When Anastasia heard of the tragedy fear overtook her. For some unexplained reason she felt that his death was linked to her. But how? She had never met Crispus and knew nothing about him until now.

As days unfolded more details emerged by way of rumors. Crispus had just won a gallant battle in Gaul against the barbarians. His soldiers were jubilant and praised him for his bravery and leadership. But soon after he was arrested and taken to Rome where he was tried and executed. The trial was secret and so was the execution. It all happened quickly. But why? Who was behind it? Only the emperor could arrest his son and order him killed. The thought was chilling and Anastasia dismissed it. She struggled to find answers, but none revealed themselves.

She wondered if Valerius knew something about it. He

had left on emperor's business. Was it related to Crispus' death? Was there something sinister about his trip? Surely not. It couldn't be, yet a sense of dread came over her. She began to question his absence. But logic told her that she worried in vain. What would Valerius have to do with his death?

As days turned into weeks, true to the emperor's order, no information was given on his son's death. All talk about him was suppressed, and nobody dared to bring up his name. It was as if he never existed.

In spite of the tensions Anastasia had moments of joy and hope. Joy when she thought of Demetrius and hope of becoming his wife. That hope persisted in spite of un-answered letters. When a ship pulled into harbor she ran to the docks praying for news. When no latter came she walked back to her lodgings telling herself one will come tomorrow. Hope never left her.

Chapter 27

With the passage of time and no sign of Valerius, Anastasia dared to hope he had changed his mind about marrying her. In her wildest dreams she even thought he may free Demetrius. People do change, she kept reminding herself.

Today, as she awoke to the rustle of the curtains from the breeze blowing through the open windows, and saw the blue skies on the horizon, she felt more hopeful than ever. Blue skies and sunshine always lifted her spirits. She dressed quickly and met her uncle for breakfast, wishing for a quiet moment with him, long overdue. The first thing she did was to tell him she had cancelled her marriage plans. She knew it would make him happy. He gleamed with happiness at hearing the news, knowing that his prayers were answered. She did not go into the details, neither did she mention Demetrius' escape, not wishing to place her uncle in a difficult position of knowing too much.

They were midway through their meal enjoying the

moment, when Florus suddenly arrived out of breath, barely able to speak.

"What is it my man?" the bishop asked sitting him down on a chair.

"Empress Fausta is dead."

"What?" Anastasia whispered covering her mouth with her hands.

"Yes, she is dead. They found her lifeless body in a steam bath."

"Steam bath?"

"In her private bath. Either she suffocated in an over-heated steam room or was scalded by hot water, they aren't sure which," Florus said.

"Where were the servants?"

"That's the strange part. She was alone, most unusual for her. Usually two or three slave girls are with her."

"Was it sudden? Was it an accident? Did she fall? Did she faint?" Anastasia couldn't hold back.

"I don't know the answers to any of these. All I know is that they carried her body out of the bath."

"Who carried her body?" the bishop asked.

"That I don't know, except that guards were seen at the site."

"Where is the emperor?"

"The emperor is secluded and cannot be reached. He has forbidden all to speak about it or mention her name, the same orders he gave when his son died," Florus said.

After a few more questions and no answers, it was

evident that Florus told all he knew. As she struggled with the tragic news, Anastasia recalled the time she had been introduced to the empress. It was at the dedication of a new chapel at the palace. She knew the empress was not a Christian and worshiped the pagan god Jupiter as well as other gods and goddesses, but she respected her husband's Christian religion and attended dutifully all Christian events and ceremonies.

Anastasia's thoughts then turned to the death of the emperor's son Crispus. Was the empress' and Crispus' deaths in some way related? Surely not. The deaths occurred close but that was a coincidence. She was making presumptions without knowing the facts. Crispus was executed for reasons unknown, and the empress' death was an accident. At one point she must have fainted, and being alone, had nobody to help her. Had somebody been with her she would have been saved. But why was she alone? Was that significant? She felt pity for the empress as well as the emperor for although she was known to be haughty and difficult to get along with, she and the emperor had been married for eighteen years, and with many children, they must have had affection if not love for each other.

That night as Anastasia lay in bed, she put aside the turmoil and tragedies that had engulfed the court, and imagined herself in the arms of Demetrius. They were on an island surrounded by blue waters and green mountains. The sky was clear and a warm breeze blew from the south.

She wore a white dress and a garland on her head, her hair laying softly on her shoulders. Demetrius had just kissed her and uttered words which she couldn't understand. She asked him what they meant, and he replied in the language that she understood. "You have just become my wife." She cradled in his embrace and closed her eyes.

Chapter 28

The deaths of Crispus and the empress had a somber effect on the court and increased tension on the already jittery court life. Everyone was on edge. The servants and slaves went about their tasks keeping their heads low avoiding eye contact, and trying not to bring attention to themselves. Officials at the court showed their insecurity by their failure to run the business of the empire, afraid to approach the emperor, leaving important tasks undone.

To eradicate the images of his son and wife from the minds of his subjects, the emperor ordered all visible signs of their existence to be removed from the palace and all of the empire, and their names erased from public records. Just to mention their names could bring about severe punishment. Their statues once revered and admired were destroyed, and the coins with their portraits removed from circulation. By denying their existence, the emperor tried to erase them from his memory and everyone else's as if they had never existed. The people asked themselves, why? What was behind their deaths that made the emperor act like that? Openly nobody spoke, but secret rumors circulated among slaves, servants, and courtiers.

The emperor increased military presence around the palace under the pretext of training the troops. Most did not question the escalation since maneuvers often took place close to the palace. Yet those with suspicious minds were aware that training took place in early spring and autumn, and not in the hot month of June. Something was amiss.

Even though Anastasia struggled with the tragic deaths, she came to grips with them, knowing that they would not alter her life. Her thoughts were on Valerius and what he might do. His absence and not knowing when he would return worried her and robbed her of peaceful sleep. If only she knew where he was and when he would return she could cope with it. She had heard that Constantia was back at court and decided to pay her a visit hoping for some news.

Making her way to Constantia's quarters she knocked on the familiar entrance, and followed the servant girl to the garden. How strange, she thought. I wanted to be rid of Valerius and today I want to know when he will return.

She heard footsteps and saw Constantia coming towards her. Her face covered with a veil, body enclosed in a long shawl, the small silhouette looked like a doll.

"What can I do for you my child?" she asked in a hushed voice, lifting her veil and sitting on the bench, motioning for Anastasia to join her.

The first thing that struck Anastasia were her red swollen eyes. It was evident she had been crying. Her face showed sadness that Anastasia had not seen before. She no longer had the empty look, rather the grief that invaded her soul was revealed on her face.

"Your Highness, I am here to ask if you know the whereabouts of Valerius. His absence, although a relief, concerns me. I am frightened of the unknown and what he may do next."

Constantia thought for a long time. She was struggling whether to speak or not. She rose, took a few steps then sat down again. Finally she took Anastasia's hand. "My dear daughter, before we speak of Valerius I want to tell you something. It's only a rumor, but rumors at my brother's court have known to be true."

"A rumor?" Anastasia whispered feeling something terrible has happened again.

"Yes, a frightful rumor, chilling and inhuman. Beyond anyone's belief."

"Beyond belief?"

"Yes, I dare not utter it lest I start to believe it. Yet believe it I must for the murder is true."

"Murder?" Anastasia said her voice trembling.

"Yes, the murder of the empress in the steam bath."

"The empress murdered? No, that cannot be. It was an accident. She fainted and suffocated. She was alone in the steam bath. I do not believe it."

"Believe it. She was murdered ruthlessly and died a

painful death, in scalding steam bath with the doors locked from outside. The servants heard her scream and pound on the door, but there was no escape."

"No escape?" Anastasia pressed her hands to her mouth.

"She was doomed to die. He wanted her dead."

"Who wanted her dead?" Anastasia asked in a hush.

"The emperor," Constantia whispered.

"The emperor killed his wife? I cannot believe it. It is too terrible to be true."

"Believe it. Her husband, my brother gave the order to kill her." Constantia said.

"But why?" Anastasia began to sob.

"Revenge for what she did."

"Revenge?"

"For her part in his son's death."

"Crispus?"

"Yes. My brother, the emperor signed his son's death warrant. He had him tried and executed secretly but the empress was behind it. Nobody talks about it and the details are scanty. But it was she who convinced the emperor to kill him."

"What did Crispus do?"

"Nothing. He was innocent of all charges. The empress accused him falsely. The emperor rushed to judgment and killed him on false testimony. When he realized his terrible mistake, that she had lied to have him killed, guilt and remorse overtook him. With his son's death there was no going back, and to expiate his guilt he killed the person who had forced it upon him. Having done one evil, he tried to correct it with another by murdering his wife who drove him to do it. It was his justice, and a way of clearing his conscience, if that would ever be possible."

"Did he confront her with it?"

"When he learned of his son's innocence his hatred for his wife had no bounds. He flew into a rage, screaming and smashing whatever crossed his path. He would have killed her but for the presence of the servants who later recounted the scene. She denied everything, but when presented with proof, admitted her guilt and begged for mercy. It was a terrible scene. She, kneeling before him kissing his feet and tugging at his robe, he, wrenching it from her, yelling and pushing her away. When he calmed down he told her to leave and take a steam bath. Whatever he told her made her believe he had forgiven her. But she was wrong. She should have known better, that he can say one thing and do another. When she went to her bath the servants were ordered not to follow her. The guards bolted the door from outside and turned the steam full blast. She must have realized at that moment that she was doomed."

"How tragic," Anastasia said. After a while she asked, "but what were the charges against Crispus? What did the empress accuse him of?"

"There are rumors and theories and all are hush hush. Some say she fell in love with Crispus and when he rejected her she accused him of rape. Others say he made advances towards her and she complained to her husband. But the real reason was succession."

"Succession?"

"Crispus was not her son. He was the emperor's first born from a previous marriage, and an heir apparent. The empress wanted her sons to succeed, and plotted to have Crispus killed. She accused him of treason, of planning to kill his father and take the throne. Knowing her husband's suspicious mind and rush to judgment, she convinced him of Crispus' guilt and persuaded him to murder. Because that's what it was. Murder of one's own innocent child, a monstrous evil act."

She paused and wiped the tears from her cheeks. "Crispus was brilliant, courageous and honorable. Everything that one would want in a son. I knew him since he was a baby and his loyalty to his father was complete. If only my brother had not rushed to judgment and waited a little longer, the truth would have revealed itself."

"But how could he justify the murders as a Christian emperor?"

"He truly believed that Crispus was guilty, and saw himself as Abraham killing his son with God's approval. His mind is warped and that's what he believed. When Crispus was proved to be innocent, his immediate reaction was to kill his wife who drove him to it. And so he did. The pagan priests told him the old gods could not forgive one murder to justify another. But the Christian God forgives all through penance so he felt safe to kill again and again knowing he will always be forgiven."

"He is a tormented man searching for peace," Anastasia said.

"It's of his own doing. Had he accepted the blame for executing his son and spared his wife in spite of her guilt, with time he would have found peace and sympathy among his subjects. But secrecy, silence, and hiding the truth will not give him peace, and posterity will call him a murderer. They will praise him for making Christianity legal, even give him the title of great, but the stamp of a murderer will always stay with him." She broke down into uncontrollable sobs then whispered, "I do love him in spite of his sins."

When she quieted down she said, "I have told you all that I know to keep you on guard. You asked about Valerius. My child, beware of him. I do not know where he is, but I feel he was embroiled in these terrible murders. How, I do not know, but it will come out. He serves the emperor in a wicked way. His greed for power has no bounds. Perhaps he and the empress conspired to kill Crispus, maybe even the emperor. It's a terrible thought but some evidence points to it."

"What evidence," Anastasia asked.

"Several commanders were executed. Supposedly they confessed to treason, but no one is talking. The military maneuvers close to the palace are also telling. The absence of Valerius is significant. Where is he? Nobody has seen him." She thought for a moment then with an urgency on her face said, "go to Bosporus my daughter where Demetrius awaits you. I will send a trusted guard to escort you on your journey. Leave before Valerius comes back and threatens you. There is trouble ahead."

"I cannot yet leave. I must think of my uncle."

"Your uncle is safe. It's you who are at risk."

"My uncle needs me," Anastasia said.

"The Christians in Bosporus will need a bishop. It could be arranged."

"He is too old and sick for change."

Constantia sighed, shaking her head. "My daughter, may God keep you safe."

The women parted. On leaving Anastasia thoughts turned from fear of Valerius to the love of Demetrius. "Where are you, my love, now that I need you?"

Chapter 29

It was the middle of July and the Council was finish-ing its business. After much discussion and emotional dialog, after ample time to speak and express their views, the bishops composed and adopted a Creed, which came to be known as the Nicene Creed. It affirmed and estab-lished that Jesus was the Son of God, true God from true God, Divine and equal to the Father, and the second per-son of the Trinity, that He always existed and was of the same substance as the Father. The Creed solidified the truth and in part read, *"I believe in one God, the Father al-mighty, maker of heaven and earth, of all things visible and invisible. I believe in one Lord Jesus Christ, the only Begot-ten Son of God, born of the Father before all ages. God from God, Light form Light, true God from true God, begotten, not made, consubstantial with the Father; through him all things were made......I believe in the Holy Spirit, the Lord, the giver of life, who proceeds from the Father and the Son, who with the Father and the Son is adored and glorified, who has spoken through the prophets....."*

With the adoption of the Creed, the teachings of Arius and his supporters were rejected and condemned, and the bishops were faced with important work of disseminating this doctrine throughout their dioceses and all Christian communities. They knew it would not be an easy task. For even though the majority of the bishops signed off on the Creed, and accepted the decision of the Council, including several bishops who had at first opposed it, there were those who remained loyal to Arius. As Bishop Caelius told Anastasia, "I am afraid that this is not the end to the conflict. It will take several generations before the controversy is settled, but this strong affirmation that Jesus is God and equal to the Father, will guide the Church into the future. We had accomplished what we came for, and I am humbled that I took part in this holy and historic event."

Anastasia had not been present when the bishops signed off on the Creed and her curiosity was aroused. "Was it difficult to get the bishops to sign the Creed," she asked.

"There were different opinions, and if it wasn't for the emperor, we may not have reached an agreement. He made a powerful speech for unity, and had to push some of the bishops to vote his way. Some of them took serious persuading, but finally the majority accepted the Creed except a few including Arius whom he exiled."

"So the emperor believes that Jesus is equal with the Father, and of same substance as the Father," Anastasia stated.

"The emperor wanted unity within the Church and was not really committed to either side. He is not a theologian and does not understand these issues. His closest advisor geared him in the right direction, and for that I thank God," Bishop Caelius said.

He paused and reflected at what he was going to say next. "But I'm afraid that considering how often the emperor changes his mind, and how easily those around him persuade him to their way of thinking, he may rethink his opinion, and reinstate Arius and those who supported him. But the Creed we have written and the beliefs we have affirmed will remain for eternity. Whatever problems lie ahead we will leave for another time. The bishops were pleased and so was the emperor that we settled the matter, because the controversy was weakening the Church and the empire."

It was late when Anastasia lay her head on the pillow. Reciting the Creed, she sensed that something extraordinary was accomplished at the Council, and that she, an insignificant girl from Rome, was a witness to this event. For generations to come, and for as long as humanity inhabited the world, this affirmation inspired by the Holy Spirit would be the bedrock of Christianity. Many things may change within the Church, different customs and traditions may be adopted, but this dogma, this doctrine will remain solid, and the Divinity of Jesus, his sameness with the Father, and His place in the Trinity was assured.

That night she put aside her thoughts of Demetrius and reflected on the Creed, and what it meant for the Christian Church. Closing her eyes she recited the Creed.

Chapter 30

As soon as the Council finished its business, Bishop Caelius and others, still shaken at the deaths of Crispus and the empress, were ready to pack their bags and leave. The secrecy in which their deaths had been handled, the removal of all signs of their lives, and the denial that they even existed, left the bishops confused and disgusted. They agreed that the emperor was responsible for the murders, yet they were unwilling to embroil themselves in the matter, and dared not speak to him about it. Considering his generosity and commitment to the Church, they felt it was wiser to leave and say nothing, lest they trigger his rage and have the Church suffer.

In spite of the widespread gloom at the court, the emperor arranged a state banquet for the departing bishops. In the emperor's throne room, couches were arranged around long tables, where the bishops reclined and slaves served them food and drink. Musicians entertained them with instruments and songs, and poets recited poetry. Slave girls in modest gowns danced and acrobats performed gymnastics. Royal jesters provided comic atmosphere and relaxed the court etiquette. Anastasia attended with her uncle, who although enjoyed himself, fell asleep as did many other bishops who were not used to rich entertainment or staying up late.

Prior to the banquet each bishop received from the emperor in a solemn ceremony a gold crucifix, chalice, new vestments, and a generous amount of money to be divided among the poor in their dioceses. As a token of his gratitude for coming, the emperor also gave each bishop a substantial monetary gift for his personal use. The bishops cherished the gifts, and after receiving them were even more reluctant to bring up the murders.

As the bishops were departing, plans were being made for celebrating the emperor's twenty years on the throne. The emperor took personal interest in organizing the festivities, and those who worked with him saw him as a happy man. Yet in spite of the emperor's outward appearance, the memory of his wife standing over him, urging him to sign his son's death warrant, tortured him without mercy. Yes, he had signed the execution order, but she had tricked him into thinking Crispus was guilty of treason.

But who else was embroiled in this act, he kept asking himself. She was not alone. She must have had accomplices. He regretted not interrogating her further. He had been livid and wanted her dead. It was a mistake. He should have grilled her until she divulged everything. But it was not too late. He will find the guilty and they will pay with their lives.

To get to the bottom of the plot the emperor conducted a secret investigation. It was a conspiracy, of that he was certain. Slowly and methodically he began to unravel the evil scheme. Those who testified falsely against his son at his trial, others who accepted bribes knowing he was innocent and said nothing, and the judges who knew his innocence yet judged him guilty, all paid with their lives. Most were not conspirators, but had gone along with the verdict to ingratiate themselves with him, to win his favors, and to advance themselves knowing his thinking at the time. In Constantine's mind, they were just as guilty as those yet unknown who plotted his son's death. There must have been a leader, and the emperor swore he would expose him.

About the time the bishops were leaving, a sad encounter happened about which only whispers were heard. Crispus' young wife and his infant son had appeared at court. She had travelled from Gaul where her husband had been stationed before his arrest and where she saw him last.

When the emperor's soldiers came to arrest her husband, they broke into their home at night, and pulled her husband from bed accusing him of treason. She screamed at them to let him go, but Crispus calmed her down and told her it was a mistake, and he will travel freely to exonerate himself. His last words to her before he kissed her goodbye were that he will be cleared, and will soon return. Holding her crying baby she believed him.

When she learned her husband had been killed, her rage was beyond words. She gathered her son, and after a long journey stormed her way into the emperor's palace. Servants heard her violent screams in the emperor's chamber.

"I don't care what happens to me. You can kill me too. But the blood of my husband and your son is on your hands. May the gods punish you for what you did, and may you meet a torturous death." She raised her baby in front of the emperor and screamed, "look at him, my son. This is your grandfather, the man who murdered your father."

"Stop, I cannot bear it," Constantine cried, turning away and covering his ears. Nausea overtook him and he spat on the ground.

The servants lifted the screaming woman and her baby and carried them away. Her screams and curses trailed behind her. Soon after, the mother and child left the court. It was rumored that the emperor compensated her for her loss and grief, bought her a magnificent villa in Gaul where her family lived, and secured her a luxurious livelihood with a large pension. He allotted a generous retirement for her parents, and allocated money for his grandson's education, promising him a high ranking position when he reached maturity.

But those who knew her wondered whether she would ever recover. Their love for each other was so deep, and their happiness so complete, that the death of one would lead to the death of the other. They had met in Gaul where she lived with her merchant family who made weapons for the Roman army. It was love at first sight. Soon after, they were married in a magnificent ceremony attended by dignitaries and commanders throughout the empire. The emperor had stood proudly by his son and his beautiful wife, and vowed to give them a glorious future.

And now a tormented soul, she walked days and nights calling for her husband, and telling her baby to avenge his father. Her hatred for the emperor was so fierce, her heart so unforgiving, that many feared she would lose her mind. They thought that her only escape from a tragic future was to become a Christian. By forgiving the emperor she would begin to recover, her pain would ease, and in time peace would enter her heart. They hoped she would find comfort in the new religion, yet her future remained uncertain.

Chapter 31

Days passed and Anastasia was at a loss. In spite of his promise to write, she had not heard from Demetrius. Her letters to him went unanswered. Every time a ship arrived from Bosporus she ran breathless, hoping for a letter or a message from a sailor, but none awaited her. Her mind wondered in many directions and all of them frightening. Perhaps he had been caught and killed. Would Valerius have had a hand in it? His spies could have learned of his escape and seized the ship before it reached land. Or maybe pirates had captured the ship. Pirates seldom released their prisoners. They make them walk the plank. Perhaps they met with bad weather and the ship sank. The ship was small and privately owned so it would not have been necessarily reported. In her despair she knew she would have to wait and pray.

It was one of those evenings when Anastasia was in her room alone, praying, thinking, and deciding what to do, that tragedy struck. Her uncle was dining with several bishops, saying farewells before they would go their separate ways. Suddenly there was a knock on the door and urgent voices coming from outside. She opened the door and saw Florus standing out of breath.

"Come with me. Your uncle is ill. He is asking for you," he blurted out.

"What happened?"

"He had just finished dinner and was feeling fine. Suddenly he grabbed his chest, groaned with pain and fell. He was gasping and almost stopped breathing, but with the grace of God regained his breath."

"Is he in the infirmary?"

"He is at the restaurant. His bishop friends placed him on a couch. He is alive, but for how long we don't know."

Anastasia grabbed her cloak. "Take me to him."

A carriage was waiting outside and she and Florus jumped into it. "Hurry to the market square and the Royal Eatery," Florus said to the driver.

The carriage left the palace grounds, and rolled through the city streets along the bank of the lake, until it reached the market square where restaurants and shops encircled the square. Anastasia's head was spinning. "Oh God, let him live," she prayed.

Upon their arrival the proprietor met them at the entrance and escorted them to a private room. In the corner of the room lying on a couch was her uncle. He was surrounded by his bishop friends who seeing her moved aside.

Anastasia approached her uncle and came face to face with him. His eyes were closed, his lips were blue, and his breathing was labored. She touched his forehead, it was cold and wet. She knelt by his side and took his hand in hers. "Uncle, it's me Anastasia."

For a minute he was silent then recognizing her voice opened his eyes. Slowly and with obvious pain he said, "I know my time has come to meet my Savior. I need to tell you....."

"Uncle, do not speak. Just rest."

At that moment a doctor who was a Greek slave came into the room. He was holding a bag. "I am the palace doctor. The emperor sent me. Please move aside."

Everyone moved including Anastasia.

The doctor bent over the bishop and pressed his ear to his chest. He felt his forehead and examined his hands and feet. They were blue. He asked for a pillow which the proprietor immediately brought, and raised his head.

After finishing his examination the doctor turned to Anastasia. "It's the bishop's heart. He has an irregular beat. It is very serious."

"Doctor, I will take him to my quarters where I can nurse him."

"My lady, you do not understand. Unless a miracle happens, his condition is fatal. He cannot be moved. I will give him medicine that will help him breathe and let him sleep, but will not cure his illness. There is little hope. He will soon lose consciousness, and then it's only a matter of time."

The doctor took out a small pouch from his bag and

asked for a cup of hot water. Pouring the herbs into the water he stirred the mixture, and bending over the bishop brought it to his lips. Half awake and panting the bishop drank it and soon fell asleep.

By that time his bishop friends had left, leaving word to be called if their colleague worsened or miraculously improved. Only Florus and Anastasia remained.

The proprietor brought in fresh linen, a wash tub, and couches for Anastasia and Florus. The vigil began.

How long her uncle slept Anastasia wasn't sure. She watched over him deep into the night until she fell asleep, exhausted and frightened. When she awoke it was light. Her uncle was awake, his lips moving in prayer. When he saw her he motioned for her to sit beside him. His voice was hoarse and his words were broken.

"My child, I must tell you something. Beware of Valerius. He is…..," he stopped and began to gasp for air, unable to continue.

"Uncle, don't talk. I know what kind of a man Valerius is."

"My child, that's not all," he struggled to speak. "It's much worse. He plotted to have….." he began to cough and blood came out of his mouth.

"Uncle, do not speak. Save your strength."

"I must speak." He coughed up more blood then relaxed. Anastasia washed his mouth. After a few minutes he said, "listen my child, Valerius plotted with the empress to have Crispus killed."

Anastasia turned white. "What are you saying? It cannot be. Valerius is evil but he is not a traitor."

"It is true. They planned the conspiracy. It's all unravelling now. The emperor knows and will soon act. The empress initiated the dreadful deed, promising him riches and power, and he complied. She did it so her son could inherit the throne, and he, to move closer to the throne. They didn't think the truth would surface." The bishop began panting and pressed his hand to his chest. "Go back to Rome, my child. Get away from here. Valerius is dangerous and who knows how far he will go." He started coughing again and this time it took longer for him to stop.

"I will not leave you." Anastasia began to cry holding on to her uncle's hand.

"My child, I will soon die. They can bury me here. But you must go home. Evidence against Valerius is mounting. I beg you to go home." His eyes were pleading.

She shook her head knowing she would never leave him. She will stay with Florus and wait for the end. Yet her inner strength began to fail. Her uncle's illness and Valerius' treachery had crushed her. She began to feel weak. Could she survive the tragedies befalling her? She must be strong. She must not panic.

She took a few minutes to calm herself. In control again, she bent down to her uncle. He was groaning and moving his lips.

"Uncle don't try to talk."

"I must. The bishops with whom I dined learned about the plot. We met to see what action to take. They were appalled about the murders and wanted to go home. I hoped to take a different path but it's too late now." He stopped to rest. Anastasia didn't know if she should let him continue or try to keep him quiet.

A few moments later with a sudden jerk the bishop raised his head. He was in pain. Then in a whisper because his voice had failed him he said, "the evidence against Valerius is mounting and soon he......"

He didn't finish and began to choke. His head fell back on the pillow. His mouth opened as he struggled to breathe, and his lips trembled. His face showed strain as well as belief that something great awaited him. Then in a final vigor of life he raised his eyes to heaven and said, *"Jesus remember me when you come into your kingdom."* Luke Chapter 23, Verse, 42. Saying that the spirit left the bishop and a peaceful expression appeared on his face as he heard Him reply ......*"Amen, I say to you, today you will be with me in Paradise."* Verse 43.

All was still. Anastasia bent over him and put her ear to his chest. His heart was silent. She closed his eyes. It was over. The uncle who raised her, the man who taught her the faith, the man who loved her as his own, was no more. She was alone, an orphan once again, and a girl in a strange land.

She was frightened and bewildered, yet she knew she must keep her wits. Instructing Florus to alert the bishops that her uncle had died, who in turn would notify the emperor, she sent a messenger to Constantia informing her of his demise. She waited until the palace doctor certified his death, and the guards removed the body to prepare it for a Christian burial. Exhausted and grief stricken, she rode back to the palace and made her way to her quarters where Constantia awaited her.

Putting her arm around Anastasia, Constantia said softly, "do not worry. You are not alone. Come to me when you are ready to talk." She lay Anastasia on the bed, and after telling a servant to bring the grieving girl a cup of soothing liquid, she waited until Anastasia fell asleep.

Chapter 32

H er uncle's funeral service was solemn and long. It took place in the palace chapel which for this occasion was draped in black. The icons and tapestries commemorating Christ's birth, crucifixion, and resurrection, reminded all whose house this was, and the burning incense paid homage to the presence of God in the highest. The emperor and his entourage, his sister Constantia, and all the bishops attended.

Anastasia who had been busy with the funeral preparations as well as her uncle's business, had not had time to grieve, even though she yearned to release her sorrow and lighten the burden of pain. At the request of the bishops she selected the hymns to be sung, the Gospel readings to be read, and made other decisions pertaining to a funeral, especially a funeral for a bishop. She chose to have a closed casket, wanting the bishops to remember him alive rather than dead.

The palace musicians played sacred songs, and the palace choir sang hymns. A bishop friend delivered a moving eulogy which made Anastasia cry. He spoke about the suffering which her uncle endured during the persecutions, how he managed to hide the sacred vessels and vestments from being destroyed, for which he would have been killed if the Romans had found them, and the chances he took in helping save Christians during these terrible times. The emperor spoke briefly, praising him for his devotion to the Church and his work with the poor. The musicians played the dirge, and the mourners followed the casket to a cemetery not far from the palace, where his coffin was lowered into the ground. Later, a marble tombstone, a gift from the emperor, was erected at his grave.

Throughout the ordeal Anastasia showed a courageous front. She attended various events celebrating her uncle's life, and received condolences from the bishops and palace courtiers. In the evenings, she labored long hours to arrange her uncle's notes from the Council meetings, and submitted them to the Council secretary. The emperor who was genuinely grieved sent her a sympathy gift of a pearl necklace, and ruled that the money which the bishop had received for his own use would now go to Anastasia. She allocated part of it for Florus' retirement in gratitude for his loyal service, and arranged his passage back to Rome.

Parting from Florus was emotional and stressful, and when the time came to say goodbye she burst into tears. A faithful servant to her uncle, himself having been persecuted, he gave up his life serving the bishop and the

Church. She provided him with a letter of reference, and he was free to search for employment, but she hoped with the money she gave him he would retire in comfort, knowing he had done his part in building the Church.

After the funeral the bishops began to disperse, each going back to his diocese. When finally alone in her quarters Anastasia broke down and sobbed. Her uncle, the last living relative of her family on whom she relied for guidance was gone. Now, without his protection from the threats of Valerius and the intrigues of the court, she was vulnerable. But most of all she grieved for the uncle who raised her, who took the place of her mother and father, and whom she loved very much. She was sad that he died before seeing Rome for the last time, the city that he loved, where he spent his life protecting the Christians and spreading Christ's Gospel. Guilt began to chisel at her conscience, and she wished she had spent more time with him. Busy and immersed in her life, she often found excuses to leave him alone, knowing he wanted her near him.

One particular time stood out in her mind. It had been a hot day in Rome. She had come home tired from work at the local church. The children she taught had been loud and mischievous. Waiting for her was her uncle eager to greet her. Instead of taking time, even a few minutes to exchange news of the day, she said she was tired and wanted to rest. He said he understood. Thinking about it now brought tears of regret. Yes, she had been tired, but all he wanted was a few minutes of her time, and she could have easily complied. It would have made him happy. He never complained about such things which were quickly forgotten. He loved her unconditionally. But now that he was dead, such moments could not be recaptured.

She stayed inside her room for three days, releasing her grief and guilt a little at a time, until the tears stopped and emptiness took over. But not for long. Strength and courage to face life's challenges filled the void within her, and gave her new resolve to find Demetrius and be free of Valerius.

Not waiting for news which may not come, she decided to take action. With the money from the emperor she booked a passage on a merchant ship sailing to Bosporus. She didn't know what awaited her there, but she knew that waiting became unbearable. She must find out if Demetrius reached Bosporus.

She bade farewell to Constantia who had tried to dissuade her from going alone. Pleading with her she said, "my daughter, do not sail into the unknown by yourself. It is dangerous for a young girl. There are many perils at sea and beyond. Let me at least provide you with protection."

But Anastasia would not listen. "I will be safer on the sea and beyond, than waiting here for Valerius to return. I will never be free of him in the empire. I must go where Rome cannot touch me. Bosporus is calling me. It is where my destiny lies."

"There is something you should know before you leave,

which may change your mind," Constantia said. "The emperor had issued a warrant for Valerius' arrest. The traitor is hiding, but not for long."

"Hiding? Where?"

"Nobody yet knows but the emperor will find him. No stone will be unturned. The emperor has mobilized all his resources to hound him down. No need to fear him anymore."

"My dearest mother," Anastasia said. "If they find him, glory to Rome. But I cannot wait and must follow my heart. I will write and be with you in spirit, until we meet again."

And so it was. Constantia sighed and accepted her choice. The two women kissed, each hoping they will meet again.

〜•〜

On the morning of her journey, Anastasia packed the few belongings she had in a canvas bag, visited her uncle's grave one more time and placed a bouquet of flowers, said goodbye to her friends, then took a carriage to the docks. Arriving at the waterfront she inhaled the ocean air. It was salty and brisk. The sky was blue and the waters were calm, ensuring a smooth sail. Even her travel sickness would not plague her. The thought of seeing Demetrius took all that away. She looked around deciding which way to go when a sailor approached her. "My lady, are you travelling to Bosporus?" he asked

"I am," she said eyeing him with caution.

He saw her concern and said, "do not worry. The captain sent me to gather the ladies who are travelling alone. There are several of you, and my task is to escort you to the ship. All is ready for departure. Please come with me." His voice was gentle and reassuring.

He took her bag and offered his arm which she refused. He smiled and said, "young ladies today want to be independent. I understand."

They walked along the waterfront passing large and small vessels until they came to the end.

"There are no more ships. We passed them all," she said beginning to feel uneasy.

He did not answer, instead he took her arm and quickened his step.

She tried to pull away knowing something was wrong, but his grip was tight.

"Sir, where are we going?" she cried trying to shake him off.

He remained silent and tightened his grip. She began to struggle, trying to free herself.

By now they were scuffling and reached a cave. She began to scream. He flung his hand on her mouth and silenced her. With the other hand he grabbed her waist and dragged her into the cave. She continued to fight as he pulled her into a dark passage. Another man appeared and pressed a kerchief to her nose. She smelt a strange odor and began to sway. Her legs weakened, her body turned limp, and her head began to spin. She felt herself fall. Rough hands caught her and dragged her deeper into the dark passage. She blinked to clear the mist in her eyes, and gave one last effort to free herself. Before losing consciousness she cried, "Oh God I'm dying, have mercy." She closed her eyes and saw no more.

Chapter 33

She opened her eyes and saw she was in a large chamber with a low ceiling. The only light came from a burning torch bolted to the wall. She was lying on a bed with soft pillows under her head. Next to her bed was a table with fruits and nuts. She felt nauseated and turned away. Her left arm felt sore and she massaged it.

Slowly she began to remember what had happened. It was so unexpected. There was a moment before her abduction when she could have escaped. But her screams came too late. There was nobody to hear her. But why would anyone want to take her captive? At first she was baffled, and then the awful truth began to unravel.

She heard footsteps and a man appeared before her. He stood in the shadows and his face was hidden. Slowly he emerged from the darkness and Anastasia knew. Before her stood Valerius.

She recognize him immediately in spite of his changed appearance. He had a beard which made him look older. His face was thinner and showed signs of stress. His eyes bulged and his lips seemed thinner and tightly drawn. His uniform was that of a Roman general, and she wondered when he was promoted. A helmet with plumes covered his forehead and ears. He had a frown on his face but it was a frown of concern, and he seemed genuinely pleased to see her.

For an awkward moment they looked at each other in silence. Then Anastasia spoke. Her voice was shaky, but the anger in her voice was unmistakable. "You have brought me here against my will. It is a crime under Roman law. The emperor will punish you for abducting me."

"Forget about the emperor," Valerius said. "His days are numbered. I intend to depose him and become the emperor."

"So it is true what they said about you. You are a traitor, and you'll die a traitor's death."

His answer was firm and his voice confident. "It's Constantine who is the traitor. By becoming Christian he betrayed Rome and Rome's glorious past. The people don't want him as emperor. They want me instead. They want the old religion back. I will give them back the old religion. I will restore the pagan gods and temples and rule from Rome."

"But you are a Christian. How can you revert to paganism?"

"I was a Christian for Constantine's sake. Now I'm a pagan for Rome's sake."

"It's not about religion it's about you. In your lust for

greed and power you became a traitor and a killer. You have no scruples, no morals. You are an opportunist of the worse kind. "

"No different than the Christian bishops. They were silent on Crispus and the empress' murders, not wishing to anger the emperor. They did what suited them best. Wasn't that opportunism?"

"How dare you compare yourself to the bishops!"

"Their silence made them complicit."

Anastasia had enough. Anger gripped her but at the same time she became frightened. With a shaking voice she asked, "how do I fit into this?"

"You will be my empress. I have loved you from the first moment I saw you. You are the only one for me."

"You are insane. Do you think I would accept you now after I had refused you before?"

Valerius was not listening. His face took on a desperate look. "Can't you understand that I love you, that I can't get you out of my mind?" he pleaded.

"Then get me out of your mind because it will never happen. I love another." She was trembling by now.

"You will never see Demetrius again," he said.

Anastasia turned white. "What do you mean?"

"Have you received any letters from him since he made his escape to freedom?"

Anastasia did not answer.

"No, I didn't think so." Valerius said with sarcasm. "Neither had he received letters from you. You see my sweet Anastasia, I have intercepted all the mail between the two of you. My soldiers seized your letters before they left port, and seized his letters when they arrived. Here are the letters from him to you and from you to him." He threw down on the table a bunch of letters tied together with a string.

Anastasia knew it was over. Demetrius was dead or captive in some dungeon, and yet she needed to ask. "Is he alive?"

"He was when he wrote the letters. But now I don't know and don't care. He is not a threat to me any more so it's not my concern."

Anastasia folded her hands in prayer. There was hope. However small she would cling to it.

A soldier in full armor came in and saluted Valerius. "Sir, your supporters are ready to fight. They are waiting for orders."

Valerius turned to Anastasia. "I must leave now to go into battle. Soon I will be the emperor and you will be my empress."

"I will never be your empress."

Valerius came close to Anastasia and she felt his breath upon her. There was sadness in his voice when he spoke. "I told you before and I'm telling you again. If I can't have you, than nobody will. I meant it then and I mean it now." He reached for her hand but she withdrew it. "As you wish my dear," he said, then turned around and left.

She was alone with two soldiers guarding her. Escape

was impossible. She felt exhausted and her head was spinning. Too distraught to think, she was longing to sleep. She reached out to the table and taking the bundle of letters placed them under her pillow. She will die with them close to her heart. Still under the influence of the drug she fell into a deep sleep.

Chapter 34

How long she slept she wasn't sure but upon awakening she felt refreshed and strong. She didn't know if it was night or day as the chamber was dark, the only light coming from a burning torch. The guards were still guarding her, but they stood away giving her reasonable privacy. A plate of fish and vegetables was by her bedside, and a fresh dish of fruit and nuts, as well as a canister of juice.

She reached under her pillow and breathed a sigh of relief. The bundle of letters was still there. By the light of the torch she picked the ones from Demetrius. They were addressed to her in care of Her Highness Princess Constantia. All of them had been opened. Anger surged within her at this invasion of privacy, but she did not dwell on it. Her heart beating with anticipation, she took the one dated first and began to read.

My sweet Anastasia:
We arrived safely in Bosporus although a storm gave us some tense moments. The natives welcomed us with a meal

fit for a king. Tomorrow we will travel to the Christian settlement located inland. They tell me that Greeks and Romans are welcome here, especially Christians who conduct missionary work. Arbeas and his fiancé send you their best. They plan to marry once we reach the settlement. My heart towards him is softening. He is sincere in his sorrow for betraying me. I struggle, yet I know I must forgive if I am to be a Christian.

I await impatiently your letter. I love you and think only of the time when you are in my arms.

Yours forever, Demetrius

With watery eyes Anastasia kissed the letter and pressed it to her heart. He was safe. He was alive. Folding her hands in prayer she raised her eyes to heaven.

She read the next letter dated several weeks later.

My precious Anastasia:

I have not heard from you. Are you still mine? The Christian community welcomed us and gave us lodgings. I am teaching in the Christian school run by missionary friars. Arbeas and his fiancé became husband and wife. I have forgiven him and feel at peace. The Christian faith is guiding us both to a godly and rewarding life. We will be baptized at Easter. Write and tell me you're still mine. I am yours forever.

Demetrius

She lay the letter aside and with a heavy heart opened his last letter.

My beloved Anastasia:
Where are you? Why do you not write? Does that mean that you are no longer mine? Are you still in Nicaea? They tell me that the Council has finished its business and the bishops returned home. Are you back in Rome? If so I pray Her Highness will forward this letter to you. My heart yearns for you. Not a minute passes when my thoughts are not with you. Write, write, write and comfort my sorrowful heart. If you are no longer mine tell me and I will treasure the moments we had.
Yours forever, Demetrius

Her heart sank. He thinks she has abandoned him. Will she ever see him again?

Suddenly there was a movement of feet and loud noises coming in from the passage. She hid the letters in her tunic and sat up on the couch. A soldier came in, saluted her and said, "you must come with me. Commander Valerius gave the order."

"Where are you taking me?" she said rising and moving away.

"I am are not at liberty to say."

"I will not go unless you tell me," she said defiantly.

"My lady, please don't make it harder. I have my orders. Nobody will harm you." He took a step towards her.

"Get away from me," she screamed backing away until she reached a wall with nowhere to go.

The soldier called out and a man came in with a kerchief in his hand. He pressed it against her nose. She tried to struggle but her head began to spin. She knew they were putting her to sleep but had no more strength to fight. "Someone help me," she cried as her body wilted.

A soldier picked her up and carried her through the passage and into a waiting carriage outside. No one was around to see her.

Chapter 35

She awoke and smelled salt in the air. She was lying on a sofa in a large room surrounded by tall pillars and a high dome. Through the opening in the ceiling sunlight spread its golden beams into the room. A table filled with fruits and sweets stood next to her. Across the room sheer curtains revealed a balcony, from which a soft breeze blew into the room.

She rose and timidly walked to the balcony. A magnificent view of the ocean blended with the blue sky. The sea gulls flying low dipped their beaks into the water in search of food. Overtaken by the beauty of the scene she forgot she was a prisoner. Yet the feeling of freedom didn't last long. She was in a fortress on a high cliff, surrounded by water on three sides, the fourth connected to the mainland by an isthmus.

Hearing steps she ran back to the room where a young slave girl curtsied, and handed her an envelope. Anastasia opened the envelope and read.

My darling Anastasia and soon to be empress:

As you read this letter I am fighting for Rome's future and our happiness. I am close to deposing Constantine and becoming the leader of the Roman Empire. My army is strong and brave. You are staying at my villa. I have given orders to my staff and slaves to treat you as the future empress that you soon will be. Every comfort will be yours. I cannot wait to have you in my arms.

Yours forever, Valerius

She threw the letter down in disgust. The man was mad. His obsession with her placed her in danger, and implied she was a traitor to Rome.

She struggled to find an escape yet she knew there was none. Guards stood outside her room, and soldiers of various ranks in full armor moved in and out of the villa, ready to fight on Valerius' behalf.

She began to prepare herself for death knowing it awaited her. Valerius' words were fresh in her mind. If he couldn't have her than nobody would. She believed him, for she would never consent to be his wife. His obsession had no bounds, and only her death would satisfy him. Will her life so full of promise come to an end? She was not afraid to die, but angry for her life cut short, of things left undone, of love unfulfilled. She thought of Demetrius and the grief she would cause him for not being with him. She mourned for her uncle but was glad he was spared this tragedy.

She wondered how she would die. Would he kill her in a fit of rage, his passion surpassing his reason, or take a sinister approach and plan her murder? Would he stab, drown, or behead her? Would he spare her pain and let her fall asleep from which she would never awake, or will she writhe and scream in agony, as poison spreads through her body paralyzing and chocking her breathing. The thoughts gave her chills. She did not want to suffer and was afraid of pain. Please God let it be quick and painless, she prayed.

More than a week had passed since she arrived in the villa, and although tortured by fears she adapted to a daily schedule. She would wake early and step on the balcony to watch the waves sweep across the cliffs. She was high above the water, and looking down wondered would she risk climbing down if the opportunity arose. The cliff was steep but with enough ledges for footing. As she looked ahead into the blue horizon, the image of Demetrius appeared beckoning her to come. It was only an illusion but it gave her courage and willingness to act.

Young slave girls, some of them still children, brought her breakfast and tried to help her wash and dress. Anastasia refused their help, explaining she could do for herself. Their eyes were swollen, projecting sorrow, loneliness and fear. The evil of slavery again showed its cruel side, this time in the form of children, snatched from their families and sent away from home. Why didn't Christianity condemn slavery, she asked herself again. Why didn't Christ forbid it? Would Rome collapse without its slaves? Who would do the work? These were concerns for the politicians, but for the bishops it should be a matter of justice.

Even though her days of captivity were peaceful, there was constant movement of soldiers and yelling of orders. She learned that the villa was the rebel headquarters, where soldiers were housed and military decisions made. As for Valerius, he was away fighting the emperor's army on the field of battle somewhere near Nicaea.

Today as she started her day, there was an unscheduled change of guards followed by much commotion. Something was happening, what, it was unclear. Anastasia seldom spoke to the guards, but when she did they answered with respect. Sometimes they even shared news with her on the glorious progress Valerius was making in dethroning the emperor. But today they gave her courteous nods and hurried bows, with fear in their eyes.

At midday the guards became undisciplined and the situation turned to chaos. Soldiers arrived confused and in disarray. Battle weary, many wounded, they looked like a defeated army that they were. As they entered the courtyard, the wounded staggered or were carried on stretches, moaning in pain. Some cried to the goddess Angerona to relieve their pain. Others prayed to the Christian God.

The servants and slaves rushed among them carrying pitches of water and linen.

A commander sitting on a white horse raised his arm and shouted, "brave soldiers, defend our new emperor with all your might. We will be victorious."

A few raised their voices and weapons. Most were silent. Their bodies haggard and beaten, their faces terrified, they knew they were traitors and what awaited them. Having given up hope of victory, they only thought of saving their skin.

Anastasia watched with fascination. As the courtyard filled with soldiers, a chariot with four horses pulled up. A commander with plumes on his helmet jumped out of the carriage. Anastasia narrowed her eyes straining to see. She moved closer to get a better view. It was Valerius.

He was covered in dust, his armor and sword stained with enemy blood. His face was grim, his eyes narrow and cold. Seeing Anastasia he approached her and bowed. "My lady, all is not yet lost. We have a strong defense here."

He took her by the arm and led her to a small room. She was too stunned to resist. He pointed to a chair and she sat not saying a word. Servants removed his armor and washed his face. She watched in silence. When they left he said, "we've had a rough fight but replacements are coming. I am certain of victory."

"Your army is beaten," she said regaining her voice. "I saw it on the men's faces. Their eyes were full of terror for the treason they committed. They will die for their crime and you drove them to it."

"Be silent. Speak only when spoken to."

"You can silence my voice but not my spirit. I will defy you till the day I die."

"You cannot defy me for you will be my wife. In a day or two you will ride with me to the palace as my empress."

"You're mad," she said with insolence. "I will never be your wife."

"Then you will die. If I cannot have you than nobody will."

She heard those words before. This time she was not afraid. "Then kill me now. I am ready." She moved closer to him and made the sign of the cross.

His face turned crimson. "Prepare yourself for death." With that he turned around and left.

Anastasia stumbled to a couch and dropped down as if already dead. So it had come to this. Death was at hand. She will never see Demetrius again, hold him in her arms, or feel his warm lips on hers.

And yet, if she were to die, wouldn't she want to fight and try to save herself? The world belonged to the living and she was alive. She must stay alert, and when opportunity arose, be ready to act. This became her goal and her frame of mind. She will not give up. And if she were to die, she will die fighting.

Chapter 36

It was the tenth day of her captivity and a few days had passed since she had seen Valerius. She didn't know if he was still in the villa or had left to fight another battle. Tonight as she lay in bed trying to fall asleep her thoughts again turned to death. She was still alive. Did that mean he might spare her? Or would he send her poisoned food when she least expected? Closing her eyes she said good-bye to the world, made her peace with God, and sent her love to Demetrius as she always did when falling asleep, not knowing if she would awake. But the will to fight for her life never left her.

Suddenly load voices awoke her, mingled with sounds of groans and painful cries. She rose from bed and tip-toed toward the courtyard which was lit by torches. To her amazement there was no one to stop her. Entering the courtyard she froze at the ghastly sight. On the floor sprawled in various positions were dead or dying rebels, some of them gasping their last breath. Their mangled bodies, the dead piled two or three high, exuded the smell of blood and torn flesh. Walking among them were Constantine's victorious soldiers, poking the dead and the dying, looking for their leader.

She stepped over the bodies keeping to the side, trying not to look down. Nobody stopped her or even gave her an inquiring look. She reached the wall surrounding the villa and peered through a small opening. Mounted officers and infantry soldiers with shields and swords stood awaiting command. So this was the end. Constantine had crushed the rebellion as he has always done.

"Where is Valerius?" Anastasia stopped a rebel who came out from behind a rock.

"He is hiding like the rest of us," the soldier said running for his life.

Her mind now turned to escape lest the victors accuse her of treason. She ran to her room and put on a travelling tunic and cloak. Looking down from the balcony, the sea, turbulent and deep, surged over the rocky coast. Knowing that boats docked by the shore, she knew the sea was her route of escape. To reach it she must climb down the cliff.

Lifting herself over the balcony, Anastasia grabbed a rock and set her foot on a small ledge. Slowly and barely breathing, searching for a foothold and clutching the rocks, she stepped down one foot at a time, her face pressed tight against the cliff.

"Don't look down, don't look down," she whispered to herself. She was midway down when suddenly her foot slipped. Barely holding on, both feet dangling in the air, she cried out, "help me God. Have mercy."

Her face bruised, her hands bloody, she swung her legs in search of footing. Finding a ridge she veered towards it, setting her feet on the ledge.

Slowly she made her way down, step by step, one foot at a time, not looking down, until solid ground was beneath her. "Thank you, God," she said kneeling down on the moist ground. "I am free."

Moonlight illuminated the coast, and looking afar she spotted a cluster of boats. She started walking towards them and came to a landing where large and small boats were docked. Five or six sailors slept nearby on thin mattresses made of seaweed. Few others sat in a circle playing dice. As she drew closer one of the sailors stood up and waited for her to approach. He was young and dressed in the clothes of a local sailor, with a short tunic and a leather belt. He was barefooted and his head was covered with a scarf. One of his ears was pierced with a ring. Hesitating if she should advance, but realizing she had no choice, she came to him and said, "I'm looking for passage to Bosporus."

"Bosporus? That's a few days journey. I don't sail there." Saying that he walked away.

In spite of his refusal Anastasia was relieved, suspecting him of being a pirate.

As she was thinking what to do next, another sailor approached her coming in from the shadows. He was older, with a long blond beard and blond hair that came down to his shoulders. His cap covered his head and his forehead. The blond hair reminded her of a northerner, perhaps from Germania, where people with fair hair and blue eyes lived on the outskirts of the Roman Empire.

"Can I be of help?" the sailor asked.

"I wish to sail to Bosporus," Anastasia said.

"Bosporus? And what's in Bosporus for a young girl like you?"

"My fiancé is there waiting for me."

The man thought for a moment. "I will take you. How much can you pay?"

She froze. She hadn't thought of the fare. She escaped with only the clothes on her back. She was about to tell him she had no money, but was willing to work to pay for her voyage, when he spoke. "I gather you have no money or jewels on you. But how can I refuse a girl anxious to see her lover? I have business in Bosporus that awaits me so you can sail with me. Come," he said pointing in a westward direction. "You can help the cook prepare the meals."

Relieved she walked beside him, passing boats and sailors until they were alone, and only the rocky coast stretched before them.

"Where is your boat?" she asked feeling a little anxious.

"It's down a little further," he said.

They walked in silence. By now the sun had risen, showing a magnificent view of the green mountains surrounding the bay. Anastasia marveled at the beauty, yet her anxiety rose. "Where is your boat, Sir?" she asked again.

"It's around the bend in the inlet."

As they walked with no ship in sight, her anguish reached its peak. She was ready to flee, it didn't matter where, when to her relief, as they made the turn, she saw a large vessel docked in the cove as the sailor had said.

Her heart lighter, her thoughts turned to Demetrius and she began to hum.

"You sound very happy," the sailor said

"Oh yes, I am jubilant. I love the man I will marry. Such love comes only once in a lifetime."

They continued walking until they reached the vessel. It was large with sails extended ready to sail.

Suddenly without uttering a word the sailor picked her up.

"What are you doing? Put me down."

The man remained silent, tightening his grip on her.

"Release me," she cried, by now frantic. Her screams echoed across the sea, but nobody heard her.

With Anastasia in his arms, he jumped on the deck, and opening the hatch to the cabin below, slid down the narrow steps. Inside the cabin he lay her on the bed. Anastasia trembled. She recalled Constantia's warning that girls travelling alone were in danger. "Oh God, let me die before he violates me," she prayed.

She looked around for something sharp, and saw a knife on a shelf by the bed. She grabbed it, and thrusting the knife at the sailor cried out, "forgive me God."

But before she could strike him, the sailor wrenched the knife from her, and pinned her hand against the pillow. She closed her eyes not wanting to see his face. "Let it be quick," she prayed. The cabin swayed, the light dimmed and everything went dark.

Chapter 37

Anastasia awoke to the sound of waves beating against the ship. She looked around her, and for a few seconds didn't know where she was, then remembering what happened sat up in terror. She was alive and well, but had she been violated? Her clothes were intact and nothing was torn. She had no bruises and no signs of roughness. She thanked God for keeping her safe, and turned her attention to the situation at hand. Why was she here? Who was that fair haired sailor who captured her but did not hurt her? She leaned through a cabin window and saw that the ship was still at bay. But surrounding it were battle ships which were not there before.

She heard footsteps descending to the cabin and a door being unlocked. A man stood in front of her, the same fair headed man who abducted her.

"Why am I here?" she asked.

The sailor stood motionless looking intensely at Anastasia. Then with a curious look on his face, asked, "don't you know me?"

"Know you? I don't know you. Who are you?"

The man laughed. "You should know who I am, but if not you soon will."

Anastasia felt a chill. She did not like surprises.

He turned around with his back to her and stood there for a moment. Anastasia's mind raced trying to place him, but she could not recall meeting a fair haired Germanic man. She kept her eyes on him, waiting for what, she did not know.

The man turned around and faced her. "Do you know me now?" In his hand he held a blond wig and beard which he waved at her.

"I can't believe," she uttered.

"Believe it. It's me, Valerius. I never gave up on you."

"You're mad, insane. They are looking for you, and will kill you when they find you."

"I know I will die. Soon the soldiers will find me. But you will die with me."

"Why?" Her eyes filled with tears.

"Because you were mine from the day I saw you, and will never belong to anyone else."

"May God, save me," she cried kneeling down and raising her hands to heaven.

"It's not going to hurt. It will be quick."

"Don't do this, Valerius. If you love me than spare me."

The sound of human voices came from outside. Valerius walked to the cabin window and pecked. The battle ships had encircled his ship, but the soldiers had not yet made a move. It was safe for a while. He pushed a large chest against the cabin door to block the entrance. In the corner he saw Anastasia kneeling in prayer.

He bent over her and his expression turned tender. "Anastasia why did you reject me? We could have had a life."

"We never had a future," she said.

"I did this for you, to make you an empress."

"You did it for yourself. Your greed for power made you what you are."

"I was always kind to you."

"But not to the one I love."

"It's always Demetrius. Even now he fascinates you. What is it about him?"

Anastasia did not answer. The noise from outside was getting louder. She knew that soon they will be discovered.

Valerius began pacing. Sweat dripped from his brow. He looked out of the cabin window. By now the emperor's soldiers stood on the decks of the battle ships. Commanders on horseback were yelling orders.

Then suddenly a voice. "We have found you Valerius. There is no escape. Turn yourself in."

"Never." His voice was defiant.

"The emperor extends his pardon. You will be a free man."

"Just as he pardoned Licinius, then had him murdered a few weeks later? Not me. I know his vengeance and what he will do."

"We will come and get you."

"The entrance is small, one man at a time. I will kill many, before you kill me."

"We will rip the ship in half. There is no escape."

"Then do it," Valerius yelled.

"We know you have the girl. Let her go."

"She dies with me."

Valerius walked away from the window and stood by Anastasia. She was shaking. Taking her by the arm, he walked her to the corner of the cabin and told her to sit. Pointing to a flask he said, "there's wine. Drink it."

Anastasia cowered and shook her head as she looked at the poison.

The sound of battle cries became louder.

Valerius picked up his sword, run his fingers along the edge, then walked to the cabin window. Soldiers were throwing planks to his ship. He knew it was only a matter of time.

He turned to Anastasia and saw her again kneeling in prayer.

"Looking at her as if for the first time he said, "you ruined me and destroyed my life."

"Do not blame me. You destroyed yourself. The evil within you brought you to this point."

"I loved you like a goddess."

"Your love was selfish. It was perverted to satisfy your needs. It wasn't good, it wasn't noble."

"Stop," he screamed. "You ungrateful creature. I should

have killed you by now." He grabbed her by the arm and pulled her towards him. Still holding his sword he waved it in the air.

"Don't do it," she begged.

With footsteps on the deck only moments remained.

Dragging Anastasia with one hand and waving his sword with the other, he reached the back of the cabin and leaned against the wall.

Soldiers with hatchets were pounding at the door. A final blow and the door fell open.

A commander stood at the threshold. "Drop your sword and let the girl go."

"She dies with me," Valerius said placing the sword to her throat.

Anastasia lowered her eyes and saw the blade against her neck, and felt its cold touch. "What good does it do to kill me? If you love me let me go," she pleaded.

"I love you but you must die."

The commander eased himself closer to Valerius.

"Don't come any closer," Valerius yelled, pressing the sword tighter against her neck. A few drops of blood trickled down.

The commander stepped back.

"Now leave," Valerius said.

"I will not leave. You will have to kill her in front of me, then I will kill you," the commander said.

Valerius began to tremble. His eyes bulged and his face became distorted.

"I implore you let me go." Anastasia turned her eyes upon her captor and saw the face of a tortured man. But there was something else that wasn't there before. There were tears in his eyes.

He gazed at her for a moment and a tear ran down his cheek. Then suddenly, his face tormented, he pushed her away. Before she had time to fall, he plunged the sword into his heart. Staggering backward, blood gushing from his chest, he dropped to the ground.

Lying on the floor immersed in blood was the man who wanted to kill her, who almost killed her. His face was white and his lips were blue. He was motionless except for an occasional jerk. His eyes were attentive, moving from side to side, searching for someone. Seeing Anastasia, his face took on a glow and he whispered, "I loved you and could not kill you. Maybe my love was noble after all." Having spoken, he gave his last gasp and died.

Someone lifted Anastasia and carried her outside. A mist lay over the beach. Through the haze, she saw silhouettes of soldiers standing at attention on the waterfront. A carriage drove up and a woman stepped out, and came towards her. Anastasia tried to recognize her but the fog blurred her face. The woman reached out, but before she could touch her, Anastasia swayed and the world rocked around her. Within seconds she fell into the arms of Constantia.

Chapter 38

She awoke, and looking around found herself in Constantia's suite. Servants were tiptoeing around her, moistening her forehead, and rubbing her arms. Her mind began to clear, and she gradually recalled the events that brought her there.

One of the servants seeing her awake left the room and soon came back with Constantia. For the first time since she first met her, Anastasia saw her smiling.

"You are finally awake, my daughter," Constantia said her face beaming.

"How long have I been here?" Anastasia asked.

"Several days. We brought you here after your rescue. Your nightmare is over. The rebellion is crushed. Valerius is dead. He and the empress conspired to depose the emperor. They organized fights and blamed them on the Christians to weaken the empire, and killed those who suspected them. They also plotted Crispus' death."

Anastasia remembered the five men Valerius killed on the way to Thessalonica, and the fights he blamed on the

Christians. "Valerius was unscrupulous, he had no con-science, yet I never questioned his loyalty to the emperor," she said.

Constantia embraced Anastasia and said, "all this is behind you. Now you must think of your future."

"I have already decided. The one I love is far away. I must go to Bosporus."

Constantia smiled. She anticipated the answer. "I know you well enough. You will follow your heart, no mat-ter what the risks. But before you leave there is one thing you must do."

Anastasia looked at her with curiosity.

"You must meet with the emperor and ask for Demetrius' freedom. If captured his future is bleak. Now that Valerius is dead he belongs to the emperor. Slaves of dead masters are the property of the crown."

"I will do as you say. May the emperor be gracious and generous towards me."

As Constantia left she said, "I will arrange a meeting with my brother, but the request for his freedom must come from you."

———

Several anxious weeks had passed, and today Anastasia sat restless waiting to see the emperor. She had risen early to prepare for the meeting, wearing a gown, a gift from

Constantia. It was long, light blue in color with a pink belt, and tied on both shoulders with pink ribbons. A dark blue shawl covered her shoulders and head.

For days she rehearsed vigorously what she was to say. She would stress Demetrius' education, his future contributions to the empire, and his good character which Constantia would vouch for. But upon reviewing her speech with Constantia, she changed all that. The emperor, Constantia had said, although generous, especially to women and slaves, having freed several of his slaves for loyal service, was a nitpicker when it came to matters of the law. And the Roman law was clear, that slaves owed complete obedience to their masters. An escape was the most grievous of all offences, next to killing the master. And Demetrius had escaped, subject to severe punishment if captured, even death. It would be wise for Anastasia to stress his loyalty to the empire. Above all, what the emperor would value most, would be his commitment to Christianity, and his willingness to evangelize wherever he went. And this was what Anastasia intended to do.

The door opened and a servant motioned her to enter the emperor's chamber. It was large with marble columns, and walls covered with carvings of Constantine's battles. The largest carving depicted the battle at the Milvian Bridge. At the far end of the room was a dais with a purple canopy. Under the canopy, on a golden throne, sat the emperor. On each side of him was a slave waving palm branches over his head.

As instructed, Anastasia walked forward, and when within a few paces of him curtseyed low. Told to keep her head bowed and wait for him to speak, she raised her eyes to see his face.

In front of her was a man whose face had grown old since the last time she saw him. His dark curly wig, meant to give him a youthful appearance looked fake, and contrasted sharply with his wrinkled face. His lips were tightly drawn and thinner than before. Although a careful attempt had been made to cover his neck, when he moved his head he exposed a double chin.

"So, you are Anastasia, Bishop Caelius' niece," he said kindly, having been told ahead who she was. "I was grieved that your uncle died, but it was a comfort to me and I'm sure to you, that he took part in the Council. His contributions had been most valuable."

"Thank you, Your Majesty, for your kind words."

"And what can I do for you, Anastasia?"

Knowing that the emperor's time was short she came right to the point. "Your Majesty, I am asking for freedom for a Greek slave who belongs to you, whose loyalty to Rome and to Christian conversion I can ensure. I ask you with deep reverence that you set him free."

"And what do you intend to do with this slave."

"I love him and wish to marry him." She cringed.

"What!" the emperor screamed. He jumped from his throne, his face crimson, his eyes glaring. "He will pay with his life for fraternizing with a Roman woman."

He came down from the dais, and muttering to himself began to pace. Assuming this was going to be a standard request for a minor favor, he was outraged that nobody had briefed him ahead.

Anastasia stood like a statue afraid to move.

Finally his anger subsided and he asked, "what is the slave's name?"

"His name is Demetrius. He belonged to Valerius and now belongs to Your Majesty."

"Where is he now?" the emperor asked.

Anastasia closed her eyes as she uttered the words. "Valerius mistreated him gravely. He escaped to Bosporus."

"What!" The emperor roared coming close to her.

She cowered in fear not knowing what to expect. Would he hit her? Would he throw her against the wall, or call the guards to arrest her? She waited.

What seemed like eternity he finally spoke. His voice was harsh and deliberate. "A slave of mine a fugitive? You may be sure when he is captured he will spend his life in the mines, and it will be a short life too." He rang a bell and a servant appeared from behind the dais. "Inform my secretary to begin immediate negotiations for his extradition from Bosporus." Turning to Anastasia he said, "the Kingdom of Bosporus is not part of the Roman Empire, but I have good relations with the king. He will send him back in chains on the next ship. And you have also broken the law by fraternizing with a slave. It you were not the bishop's niece you would be severely punished."

So this was the end. She could hardly breathe. Her face turned white. How long will this nightmare continue? Has God forsaken her?

She will make one last effort. Let the words fall as they may. She had nothing to lose. She will speak from her heart. "Your Majesty, if you only knew the tortures Demetrius endured, your heart would melt. Demetrius escaped to shield himself from the tyranny of a Roman commander, a traitor at that. He had no choice. It was either death or escape. Nobody should suffer the way he did, but thousands do. As a Christian emperor, you know that life is precious, and yet Christians kill innocent people. This paradox among the Christians is a tragedy. Killing is a crime in the eyes of Christ. Slavery and torture are immoral, and both should be outlawed."

Realizing she was speaking to the emperor she stopped abruptly. Had she gone too far? She waited a moment, and when silence ensued she said, "Your Majesty, I beg you, have mercy on Demetrius. Punish me not him."

Constantine sat back on his throne and looked at the girl before him. Who did she think she was, lecturing him on how he should govern? He was the anointed one, the one chosen by Christ to rule a great empire and make it Christian. He can do no wrong.

And yet a menacing thought reemerged once more. He had killed again and again to keep his empire. He had tortured and purged his enemies as well as the innocent. He murdered his relatives, his wife and beloved son. Yes, even his brave and loyal son, his first born, whom he promised his mother to protect. Tears trickled down his cheeks. What had he done? Who had he become?

The words of Jesus rung in his ears, as he recalled the Beatitudes that the bishops often quoted from the Gospel of Matthew, Chapter 5, Verse 7. *"Blessed are the merciful, for they will be shown mercy."*

Had he ever shown mercy? He couldn't remember. He looked at the girl in front of him. Young, courageous and in love. He once had a wife that he loved, and their son Crispus was their joy. As his career blossomed and his ambition climbed, he divorced the woman he loved to marry the emperor's daughter. The power that she brought him fulfilled his dreams, making him caesar and later an emperor. Yet what price did he pay for what he had accomplished? His wife and son dead, his sister's husband and her young son murdered as they slept, all by his order. Did he regret his evil deeds? He did not want to think. He couldn't bear the pain. As he looked at Anastasia, the humble girl pleading for mercy, he wondered if he showed mercy, would that redeem him before Christ who gave him so much? He needed redemption to save his soul, and this was an opportune moment. Yes, he will show mercy and more for the sake of his soul.

"Young woman, as Demetrius' owner, I exercise my authority to set him free, and as emperor I decree him worthy to be a Roman citizen," he said.

Anastasia could hardly believe his words. Her eyes

filled with tears of joy. Gratitude radiated from her face. "Your Majesty, I will forever be grateful for what you have done. May the Lord Jesus Christ bless you and watch over you." She curtseyed and left.

The emperor walked to the balcony and gazed at his empire that stretched before him. Did Christ look at him with favor now that he had shown mercy, forgiven his slave, and made him a citizen? Did these good deeds gain him grace in the eyes of the Christian God? He hoped so. With his deathbed baptism and his good deeds, he should enter immediately the Kingdom of Heaven. He felt cheerful and confident. After cancelling Demetrius' extradition order, he left the throne room, and letting the robe slide from his shoulders, made his way to the baths. The slaves scrambled to catch the robe before it fell to the floor.

Chapter 39

Dawn was breaking as Anastasia looked out on the sea stretching before her, and watched the waves hit against the bow of the ship. She was finally sailing to the Kingdom of Bosporus, and the image before her was Demetrius. She had bought passage on a merchant ship carrying wine as its cargo, and the sweet aroma from the wine made sailing pleasant.

A storm had delayed her departure, and she had waited with impatience for it to pass. The winds had been treacherous and the waters turbulent, preventing all ships from leaving the harbor. Finally the weather broke, and the captain announced it was safe to sail.

While she waited out the storm, questions arose in her mind. Will the emperor fulfill his pledge to set Demetrius free? Knowing his history of breaking his word, she struggled to keep faith, and prayed that he will do what he had promised. True to his word the emperor sent her Demetrius' certificate of freedom and a document proclaiming him a citizen of Rome.

Her joy was bittersweet for she did not know if Demetrius was still hers. What will she find on the other side of the sea? Did he still love her and proclaim her his wife, or has the separation built a bridge between them that will be awkward if not impossible to cross? If upon her arrival she is left alone, what should she do?

She recalled Constantia's words of encouragement before her departure. They were standing in the harbor before she boarded, both in tears, clinging to each other.

"You must have faith that he is waiting for you. True love does not fade in absence," Constantia had said. Saying that she squeezed a pouch into her palm. "Take this. Let it give you security and independence. Be what your heart tells you to be. Believe in yourself and do what you want, and let no one tell you otherwise."

Anastasia had opened the pouch and looked inside. Emeralds, pearls, sapphires, rubies and nuggets of gold glittered within. Gold bracelets, rings, broaches, and earrings lay waiting to be worn. Amongst the jewels a large diamond, polished and cut in a shape of a heart, sparkled before her. She could hardly believe what she saw. 'I cannot take this Your Highness," she had said. "You are too kind, but these are not for me."

"Anastasia, I have taken you as my daughter, and as a mother I bequeath these to you. I have no one else. My son is dead never to have a bride. Unless you take them, they will find their way into a greedy man's pockets. Take these. You may need them someday."

Anastasia thought for a long time. Finally she had said, "I will take them and use them for the good of others." She sealed the pouch and placed it in her tunic pocket. They kissed and embraced knowing it was for the last time.

———◈———

As dawn turned into day, Anastasia took time to acquaint herself with the ship. The sailors were free Greeks and Armenian, few Christian, most of them pagan, who questioned the strange religion that recognized only one God. The captain was Greek with years of sailing, who projected wisdom and self-confidence. He was demanding but fair, and paid the sailors well. Having made this trip many times he knew the route and the sea. And as many owners of merchant ships do, he took on passengers for additional income.

Anastasia made friends with the passengers, who like herself sailed to a new life in a strange land. They were poor, mostly women, travelling with young children to reunite with their husbands who had gone ahead. How happy the families will be, she thought, when they are reunited. She hoped the same awaited her.

It had been a pleasant sail so far. The sea was calm, the sky blue, and the passengers happy anticipating their arrival in a few days. They made merry by dancing and singing, even the captain joining the festivities.

It was midway through the journey when suddenly without warning everything changed. The passengers had just finished breakfast when the captain made an urgent call. "Pirate ship ahoy!! Everyone below. Pirate ship ahoy!! Everyone below."

Children began crying as mothers with terrifying faces grabbed them and scrambled below.

Anastasia looked to the horizon, and saw a vessel hoisting a black flag with a large skull and crossbones. It was approaching at a high speed. Within minutes it would be by their side.

One of the sailors with orders from the captain hurried below deck, and began hiding the children in empty boxes and overturned dinghies, deep in the bowel of the ship. The children cried and he turned to the mothers. "Keep them quiet. If discovered they will be taken and sold. If they find one child it is over for all. They will search the ship until they find every single one."

The mothers themselves in tears comforted their children until all were silent. "Do not cry and keep your eyes shut. It will soon be over," they told the little ones. Anastasia hurried about helping those in need, and reassuring the mothers that all will be well. "God is with us, He will not abandon us now," she said.

The captain came below and being satisfied that all was quiet said, "good, let's hope it stays that way."

"Are we in danger too?" Anastasia asked, surprised that only the children were being hidden.

"The pirates prefer children ages four and above. They are a valuable commodity. They take them aboard their ship and keep them frightened, so they stay obedient and easy to control. At the next port they are quickly sold into slavery, and bring good money. Besides, they don't eat much. The adults may resist so they usually kill them. Defiance is common among the captives, and who wants a rebellious slave? Furthermore, the cost of feeding them is high."

Anastasia felt a chill. Most of the children were within that age. Only a few were babies. "Does this happen on every crossing?" she asked.

"No. This is unusual. The pirates must be hungry and in search of easy cargo. We will have to hand over all the barrels of wine."

Anastasia thought for a moment. "Captain, can't we outrun the pirates?"

By now tired of questions, the captain looked at her with annoyance and his answer was sharp. "That's impossible. Their ship is much faster than ours."

He turned his attention to the passengers and ordered all to assemble on deck. When all were gathered he said to them, "we will not fight the pirates. There is no use. We are outnumbered. If we fight and lose of which I am certain, they will show no mercy. Before they kill us they will torture us as punishment for resisting. Walking the plank is their way of showing mercy. The best I can hope is that they will quickly take the cargo and leave. So I order that nobody resists and nobody speaks. Is it understood? I will speak with the pirates, and only I. Hold your heads low and pray or pretend to pray, especially you Christians. Most of these thugs are pagans, but they seem to revere the Christian God. I hope that their captain has some conscience." After finishing his speech he ordered the wine to be brought to the deck for smooth and quick handover.

The group knelt and waited. The Christians began to recite the Lord's Prayer. The children so far were silent.

The pirate ship pulled alongside, and suddenly stamping of feet and loud voices penetrated the calmness of the sea. The pirates danced and shouted battle cries, swinging their swords, axes, and daggers high above their heads. When the cries subsided, they threw hooked ropes into the merchant ship. With their daggers and knives between their teeth, they climbed the ropes using their legs and hands with amazing skill, and quickly landed on the deck. Anastasia watched with fascination.

There were about thirty of them, outnumbering the sailors three to one. Their loose and shabby trousers reached their knees, and their checkered shirts were belted at the waist. Most had colorful bands around their foreheads and scarves on their necks. Earrings with sparkling stones clipped their ears, and a few had rings in their noses. Among them was the captain. As they landed on the deck they lifted their weapons ready for combat. Seeing no resistance, the captain raised his arm, and with a deep and commanding voice turned to the pirates. "Lower your weapons, my friends. The sailors on this ship will not fight."

He was tall, the tallest of the pirates, with a clean shaven face, and long curled mustache that reached his ears. It was easy to pick him as the captain. He looked and sounded like a leader. His long black hair was pulled back and tied with a red ribbon. The clothes he wore were finer than his crew's. The dark blue trousers were made of silk, with a matching flared jacket extending below his hips. Under his jacket he wore a white shirt, and red waistcoat with jeweled buttons. His triangular hat held a red feather that came to his cheek, and the one earing he wore sparkled with a ruby that hung long from his left ear.

He stepped forward and gave out a hearty laugh, the kind that implies satisfaction and anticipation of good things to come.

From the first words he spoke Anastasia knew he was not the typical illiterate sailor, who turned pirate in the hope of becoming rich. His language was refined and his behavior cultured. Yet he left no doubt that he was a pirate, and ready to steal the cargo.

He approached the ship's captain and bowed low, holding a double edge sword, swinging it in welcome. "It is with pleasure that I greet you captain. My name is Odysseus." He chuckled. "You must guess it's not my real name. I am here on business but you know that already," he said with humor.

The captain did not answer. He knew they were here

for the cargo and thought it best to be silent.

Hearing no reply Odysseus continued. "Looking at your passengers I see that they are poor, so I'll not search them but only take the cargo. Be thankful that I'll spare them. Today is your lucky day." He laughed in a friendly manner but the tone of his voice was serious.

"My cargo is wine. The barrels are on deck. Take all and let our ship sail."

Odysseus walked to the barrels and poured himself a cup. "Good wine. It will bring a pretty sum." He motioned to the pirates to start moving the cargo.

The passengers were kneeling and praying. One woman was close to breaking and Anastasia embraced her. "Do not show your fear or they will get suspicious."

When the pirates had finished moving the barrels of wine, Odysseus gave the order. "Go and check below." He turned to the captain and said with a chuckle, "I never leave a stone unturned," and laughed again.

Anastasia held her breath and prayed. "God, keep the children quiet."

"I'll go down with them," the captain said taking a step.

"No need. They can find their way."

"I insist."

"And I insist that you stay on deck." Odysseus lifted his sword, and as he did the pirates came forward with weapons raised.

The captain retreated.

They ransacked the cabin, their yells and curses carried

to the deck. Anastasia trembled and prayed for the children.

Suddenly a child's cry echoed across the deck. Climbing from below was a pirate holding a crying child by the collar. The boy was about four years old and calling for his mother. His little legs dangled in the air, and he swung his arms before him. Seeing her child the mother rushed to him and tried to grab him away. The pirate pushed the woman aside, and she fell to the ground screaming for her child.

What followed was a sight that brought fear to the ship's crew and panic to the mothers. As the pirates emerged from below, each carried two screaming children by the collar. When all were on deck, twenty terrified children huddled together. Seeing their mothers they rushed to them, but the pirates, swinging leather whips pushed them back. The mothers wailed, and were kept at bay by brutal blows.

"So, you have tried to fool me. You didn't tell me about the children," Odysseus shouted glaring at the captain and his crew. His face turned red, and he brandished his sword at the captain. "As punishment you will all die, except the children who will be sold."

The pirates surrounded the captain and his crew, and pushed them to the edge of the deck.

The captain pleaded. "We are two days from Bosporus. Let the mothers, children, and my sailors sail to land. Then kill me and take my ship."

Odysseus laughed. "Thank you for your offer but that's

hardly a bargain. Your ship is worthless. It is slow and in need of repairs. We'll sink it. Only the children will come with me. They will make us rich. Don't worry. We'll take good care of them until they are sold and....."

Before he could finish a woman ran to him and fell on her knees. "I beg you, let our children go. Take us or kill us, but let our children go."

"Lady, as much as your pleading affects me, I am a business man, and you and the others are of no value to me. The sooner I get rid of you the better for me." He looked at the passengers and said, "I could torture you for trying to fool me, but I have a heart." He laughed as he placed his hand on his chest and tapped it a few times. "So I'll make you walk the plank."

Anastasia listened, her face wet with tears, yet courage in her heart. It was now or never. With a firm step she approached the pirate. "What would it take for you to let the passengers and crew go free?"

Odysseus looked amazed.

Anastasia repeated her question. "Sir, what would it take for you to let the passengers and crew sail free?"

He began to laugh. "Lady, you must be joking. It would take heaven and earth, that is if there is a heaven."

"I am serious. What would it take?"

He laughed again, genuinely amused. "Lady, you don't seem to understand. Nobody has the means to buy this kind of freedom."

"I'm still curious. At what price would you set us free?"

Odysseus became irate. "Look lady, it would take gold and jewels to let you go free. And even then I'm not sure."

She reached into her tunic pocket and felt the pouch that Constantia gave her. Grasping it tight she asked, "Sir, are you an honorable man?"

"Honorable?" He looked amused. "Sometimes, not always. When I choose to be."

"Sir, you're an educated man. In your past you may have had a wife, a home, maybe even children before you turned to piracy. I'd like to make a deal with that man from the past." She waited holding her breath.

"And what have you to offer?" He laughed.

"As an honorable man will you honor a deal?"

"If I choose to be honorable."

"Do you choose?"

Odysseus laughed again. "Yes. But only if the price is right."

She went as far as she could. Now she had to deal.

"Come with me," she said to Odysseus. They walked to an empty barrel. Slowly she took out the pouch from her pocket and emptied the contents on top of the barrel. As she did, hundreds of lights glowed with brilliance. Among them the large diamond cut in the shape of a heart.

Odysseus gasped in unbelief. He held up an emerald, the largest one, and examined its transparent green hue. "Magnificent," he said. He picked up the sapphires and pearls and admired them as if hypnotized. Taking a gold ring set with three rubies of different shades of red, he placed it on his finger. "What luxury, what a feeling of ecstasy," he said closing his eyes. After examining the jewels and the gold, he reached for the heart shaped diamond and rubbed it against his shirt. It was as if he went into a trance, such was the look on his face.

When his pleasure had reached its peak, Odysseus turned to the pirates. "What do you think, my friends? Do we let the passengers and the crew sail?"

The pirates, who had been staring at the treasure shouted in unison, "let them sail, let them sail."

Once again he ran his fingers through the treasure and smiled broadly, then placed each jewel in the pouch, one by one. When he picked up the heart shaped diamond, he held it longer than the others as if not wanting to let go. Closing the pouch and tucking it safely in his pocket, he addressed the captain and the passengers.

"You have heard the voice of the pirates to which I add my vote. We will take the cargo and the gems, and you are free to sail. I will leave you two days' supply of food and water. It's enough to reach Bosporus."

He walked over to Anastasia and looked at her intensely. It was a kind look, a little curious. Speaking softly he said, "you have made us very rich. I am most grateful. I bid you farewell and good fortune." Taking her hand he kissed it, and as he did he slipped something into her hand. As he walked away he laughed cheerfully, and ordered his crew to leave the ship, and himself jumped over the railing.

Anastasia opened her hand and saw the heart shaped

diamond sparkling on her palm. What made him do it? Was it guilt? Was it chivalry? Whatever it was, a feeling of gratitude came over her. There was some good in this man after all, and she wondered what made him turn to piracy. She placed the diamond in her kerchief and hid it in her tunic.

She watched the pirate ship drift away, and the black flag with crossbones and skull being lowered. As she stood watching the ship, she realized a crowd of cheering people had surrounded her. Strong arms of the sailors lifted her in the air and carried her around the deck. "Thank you," the people cried with tears in their eyes and smiles on their lips. "Thank you for saving our lives."

Anastasia's heart melted. It was Constantia that saved their lives, and she intended to let them know. "Listen to me," she cried still in the air. "Your gratitude belongs to Constantia, the emperor's sister. She gave me the jewels to use them when needed, and the need was now. Her kindness and generosity helped us, and we in turn must help others. That is the way we repay the debt. As you start your lives in Bosporus, remember the good that was done to you, and in turn do good to others."

And she will do the same. She will find a way to repay the debt. How, she didn't yet know. As she looked out to sea, and saw the pirate ship now a speck on the horizon, she felt that the heart shaped diamond that Odysseus had left her, was linked to repaying her debt of gratitude to Constantia.

Chapter 40

The sun was just rising as the shores of Bosporus came into view. Birds circled the ship, and from the distance outlines of a busy port became visible. Workers loading and unloading cargo, boats docking or setting sail, people dickering with merchants for goods, all confirmed what Constantia had said about the city. It was a thriving port that went back centuries before the birth of Christ. Many kings had ruled this important kingdom that nestled between the narrow straits connecting two seas. Majestic public buildings and luxurious villas along the shore gave evidence to its wealth and prosperity.

As they approached the harbor, lines of people welcoming the ship awaited them. They waved their arms and pushed forward for better view. The passengers on the deck strained their eyes in search of familiar faces. They held their children high, who with great excitement waved their hands, and called for their fathers with great jubilation.

As Anastasia watched the happiness around her, she

wondered what would she find when she steps on the shore. Will Demetrius be waiting and take her in his arms?

The ship pulled into harbor and the passengers disembarked. Wives ran to their husbands, husbands to their wives, kissing and embracing, children cuddling between parents. What joy!

Anastasia stepped ashore with her bag around her shoulder and mingled with the passengers, saying goodbyes and wishing them well. As the crowd began to thin, only the merchants and sailors remained. They were loading wheat, fish, and slaves for transport to Rome. Again, the injustice and cruelty of slavery struck her as before.

A young woman slave, half naked stood on the block, her long hair concealing her breasts. Her bent head, shoulders slumped, she could not hide the tears that fell down her cheeks. A few feet away, a small boy about six years old stood crying and calling for his mother. A guard walked up to him and smacked him across the face. It was intended to make him stop crying, instead it made him cry even more.

She watched the merchants bid for the little boy and turned away unable to bear it. Suddenly she turned back and walked up to the block. As the bidding continued, the little boy exhausted from crying began trembling, his wide eyes swollen and full of horror.

When the last bidder called out his bid, Anastasia stepped forward, and taking the heart shaped diamond out of her pocket raised it high. "I bid this diamond for the boy."

The people stared at her in shock yet remained silent. The auctioneer repeated the bid three times, and when no more bids came in, he sold the child to Anastasia.

She gathered the trembling boy and pressed him to her breast. "I will be your mother now. You are free and safe." The boy grabbed her neck and clung to her unable to stop crying.

As she cuddled the boy she took one last look at the slave girl. The girl was still slumped and the bidding continued. When the final bid was made she saw the girl taken away. She felt helpless. How she wished she could have helped her. She prayed that the person who bought her would be kind.

She sat with the boy in her arms deciding what to do. From the letters Demetrius sent her, she knew there was a Christian settlement, and she made up her mind to find it. Would she find him there? Was he still hers?

She was about to rise when someone touched her from behind. It was a gentle tap and she felt the warmth of the hand. She turned around and saw a man. She blinked and rubbed her eyes gazing at the face before her.

"My God, is it you Demetrius?" she whispered breaking into sobs.

He gathered her in his arms, and a surge of emotions poured out from within her. When she had quieted he said, "there was not a day when my thoughts were not with you. I don't know what would have happened if you had not arrived."

Snuggling against him she felt his beating heart. As their lips joined so did their hearts.

"I almost thought you had forsaken me not seeing you when I arrived," she said.

"Every time a ship came into port I was waiting for you, and every time my heart dropped with grief. And this time my carriage broke down and I was delayed."

"It was meant to be. God willed it this way." She brought forth the little boy and explained what she had done. "If you hadn't been late we wouldn't have this beautiful child."

Demetrius picked up the boy and spoke few words in Greek. The boy smiled and started chattering back. "He is Greek," Demetrius cried with joy. "How can I ever thank you for bringing him to me? You have made me a very happy man."

"All I ask is that you be a father to him," she said.

"I am already," he answered. Then taking Anastasia by the arm he led her to the carriage. "I have made a life for us here in Bosporus, in the Christian community. We make our living by growing wheat and making wine, and exporting them to Rome. Did you know that we make the best wine in Bosporus and can hardly fill the orders? With the sales we make we have more than enough to feed our people, with plenty to spare."

"And Arbeas? How is he and his bride?"

"A baby is on the way. They are very happy."

The carriage left the harbor, and Anastasia admired the landscape surrounding the blue sea. As they rode inland the road was no longer paved, and the carriage having no springs made a difficult ride. But all this was forgotten by the joy that both felt at being together. The boy sat between them and as she stroked his head, she reminded him that now he had parents.

It took two hours to reach the settlement. As they approached the village, rows of wooden huts lined the road, ending at the center of the hamlet, where vendors sold produce, grain, and wine in brightly decorated kiosks. Mingled amidst the kiosks were small eateries, where freshly cooked meals were prepared and sold to customers. It reminded Anastasia of Rome where cooking in the wooden apartments was prohibited because of the threat of fire, so most Romans ate their meals at public snack bars. The aroma of hot stew filled the air, so they stopped and ate lunch of sausages, stew, and pie. Having eaten they continued on for a little longer, until they turned a corner and stopped.

"This is our church," Demetrius said pointing proudly at the building with a steeple. "Our Christian community is growing. The friars are busy preparing people for baptism. I and many others will be baptized at Easter. We have a little school at the back of the church where I teach the children and adults to read and write. Next year I will teach them the arts and sciences, and acquaint them with the Greek way of life. And when I'm baptized I hope to become a minister of the Church. It's a rewarding life, and now that you are here it will make me whole." He took her hand and kissed it.

After a moment of reflection Anastasia said, "I also want to be part of the young Church, to nurture it, guide it, and to participate fully in its work and mission. I want to evangelize, baptize, and bring people to Christ."

"Will you still be my wife and mother of my children?" Demetrius asked, cautiously.

"I can and want to be all three, a wife, mother, and a minister of the Church. God did not preclude women from priestly duties. He preached equality. Just read St Paul's letter to the Christians in Rome, Chapter 16, Verse 1. *"I commend to you Phoebe our sister, who is also a minister of the church at Cenchreae, that you may receive her in the Lord in the manner worthy of the holy ones,....."* Or his letter to the Galatians, in Chapter 3, Verse 28. *"There is neither Jew nor Greek, there is neither slave nor free person, there is not male and female; for you are all one in Christ. Jesus."* And were not women, including Jesus' mother present in the upper room after Jesus' Ascension, as stated in the Acts, Chapter 1, Verse 14. And also in the Acts, Chapter 18, Verse 26 didn't Priscilla and Aquila explain the *"Way of God"* more accurately, clarifying Jesus's teaching to Apollos who was preaching in the synagogue. And think of Mary Magdalene, whose faith led her to become Jesus' disciple, as He travelled from town to town and village to village.

Didn't she stay with Jesus at crucifixion when all the others ran away in fear, and wasn't she the first person to see Jesus after his resurrection? Surely Jesus intended women to be ministers in His Church. " She caught her breath wanting to cite more, but realized she had been carried away and had made her point, although to Demetrius it wasn't necessary.

They passed the church just as the faithful were leaving the service. Men and women were waving goodbye to each other, and the friars were collecting the children for school.

To the right of them a public bath was being constructed. "The people donated the funds and there is much excitement about it. We expect it to be ready in two months. There will be a ceremony and a dedication," Demetrius said.

All along the road masons were building new homes. Further away from the road, workers were loading barrels of wine and bushels of wheat on carts for shipment to the harbor.

"Workers are much in demand and immigrants are coming by the hundreds. We welcome them with open arms. They contribute to the growth and welfare of our village, and because of them we are a prosperous community. I was an immigrant and they welcomed me, and now you are an immigrant too," Demetrius said.

Anastasia recalled the words of Christ in the Gospel of Matthew, Chapter 25, Verse 35. "*For I was hungry and you gave me food, I was thirsty and you gave me drink, a stranger and you welcomed me, naked and you clothed me, ill and you cared for me, in prison and you visited me."*

As she watched the people at work she knew they will be rewarded. But sadness overcame her as she thought of the young slave girl on the bidding block. She will be exploited and will have to work hard, and never enjoy the fruits of her labor. She was condemned to toil for the benefit of her master until her last breath. She wondered who bought her, and will she find kindness in her captivity.

As the image of the girl stayed with her, an idea began to emerge. The heart shaped diamond that Odysseus had left her saved a little boy from slavery. But it was only one life. There were hundreds of others who would never be free.

Her idea took form and she leaned towards Demetrius, enthused. "When this child became mine there were others whom I could not help. I felt helpless. But now I feel there is a way. Suppose the surplus money that the community earns is spent on buying the slaves in Bosporus? Wouldn't that be a worthy cause? What use is money unless it's put to good use? And what better use than giving people freedom and dignity? They will contribute to the community, and their labor will enrich this settlement." She paused trying to contain her zeal. "I realize I cannot eliminate slavery. It may take centuries to change human thinking. But let's begin now and do our part, however small. And we can start in Bosporus. What do you think?"

"Who knows better than I the cruelty of slavery," Demetrius said. He rolled up his sleeves and revealed the scars left by the chains. "These marks on my wrists and others on my body are legacy of slavery and human brutality. I was free before I became a slave, but many are born slaves and die slaves. I will work with you and help convince others to help eliminate slavery in Bosporus."

The carriage turned and stopped at a house at the end of the road. It was made of wood with a chimney and two windows in front. A wide door gave entrance to the house, and above was a sign that read *"All are welcome in the name of Christ."* Several trees in the front provided shade.

"This is our home," Demetrius said pointing with pride. "The Christian community helped me build it."

She gazed at the house and sensed the love with which it was built. Pressing her cheek against his chest she heard his heartbeat. Every beat was a token of love. She was home and her love was with her.

Chapter 41

And so Anastasia and Demetrius began their life together as husband and wife. Preceding the wedding, Demetrius was officially made a free man and proclaimed a Roman citizen as ordered by the emperor. He received certificates of freedom and citizenship, and proudly displayed them for all to see. A Roman magistrate representing the emperor was present and officiated at the ceremony.

They were married in church in a simple ceremony, with Arbeas and his wife as witnesses, and the whole congregation rejoicing. According to a Roman custom, Anastasia wore a long white silk tunic over which a yellow robe swept gracefully below her knees. Her shoes also yellow were made of soft leather. Her hair was curled and lay on her shoulders. On her head she had a garland of flowers and a red veil that reached her feet. Demetrius wore a short white tunic and a blue toga. His dark hair was trimmed and neatly combed.

The bishop glowing with pride at seeing yet another

couple making their wedding vows in a Christian church, officiated at the ceremony. When he asked the bride and groom to join hands, their hearts also joined and melted into one.

"I take you, Demetrius, as my husband, with all my love and care, and will be faithful to you always," Anastasia said looking into his brown eyes.

"I take you, Anastasia, as my wife, with all my love and care, and will be faithful to you always," Demetrius said squeezing her hand.

They exchanged rings and as they did, Demetrius' eyes moistened and a tear drop rolled down his cheek. It looked like a pearl. Of all the jewels she had ever seen, this one was most precious to her. The bishop blessed the couple, and asked them to kneel in front of the statue of the Virgin Mary.

"Your first act together as husband and wife is to pray together," he said joining them in prayer.

After the service a small celebration followed, with food, wine, music and dance.

When the celebration was over the whole congregation processed to their home, with musicians playing the flute. According to a Roman custom, two young boys escorted Anastasia, each holding her hand. Demetrius followed escorted by two young girls. When they reached the house Demetrius picked her up, and carried her over the threshold, following yet another Roman custom.

And so they settled in their home, and began working

for the good of the community and the emerging Christian Church. When Anastasia found that she was to be a mother, their joy and gratitude had no bounds. Their adopted son eager for a brother or sister helped them prepare for the new arrival.

At Easter Demetrius was baptized, and few years later the bishop ordained him as minister of the Church. "I am blessed to be able to serve the Church and have a family," Demetrius said.

Anastasia was ordained as minister in her own right, conducting baptisms, weddings, and funerals. When her daughter was born she thrived in her roles as mother, wife, and minister of the Church. She prayed that her daughter when grown would have the same choices, but remembered her uncle's words:

"......*I hope there is room for women to be leaders and ministers of the Church. Since the early days of the Church the women have served admirably. But I'm afraid this is dwindling, and a new order will follow. It is unfortunate that since Christianity became legal, women have been pushed aside, and men have taken over. But some day women will return to serve the Church to the fullest, as priests and bishops, not in my lifetime, and not for a long time, but some day, I firmly believe it.......*"

As she pondered these words she believed that the Church will grow and change amidst the struggles and sins of the people.

A pinnacle of their joy was the fulfilment of the

promise they both made on the day of their reunion. After much persuasion and hard work, the Christian community voted to buy slaves that passed through Bosporus with the surplus income. At first only few were set free, but within a few years, all slaves brought to Bosporus were bought en masse by the Christians and settled in the community. Bosporus became a slave free kingdom. Anastasia arranged for their housing, education, and health care services. Children were given special attention to prevent trauma. "We do our part, however small, to change the world for the better," she used to say.

As years went by they welcomed two more children, a son and daughter, and adopted two more sons. They grew vegetables and sold them at the market, and Demetrius continued to teach at the parish school. They prospered and kept what they needed, and gave the rest to the ones less fortunate. "What good is money if not used for a worthy cause," Demetrius often repeated to those who did not understand.

One of Demetrius' proud achievements was the opening of a library at the church. With the church's blessings and financial support, he bought books from Rome and Greece and developed a fine collection on religion, arts, and the sciences. Inhabitants from all of Bosporus used the library. Even the pagans, some of them high ranking officials who looked with suspicion at the Christians, came to enjoy it. "If we welcome all citizens and let them get to know us, they will learn that we, Christians, are ordinary citizens just like they, except that we believe in one God, Jesus Christ," Demetrius said.

It was on a day when Demetrius was visiting a sick parishioner that Anastasia received the bad news. A girl came running half in tears. "Your husband has collapsed and has been taken to the church."

Anastasia ran to the church and found her husband lying on a couch in the church office, surrounded by friends, parishioners and his children. He was gasping for air and rubbing his chest trying to ease the pain. Sweat run down his cheeks. She knew the symptoms. It was his heart. In the last few months he had been tired and often had pain and nausea.

Seeing Anastasia he spoke. His voice was rasping and his words broken. "My darling wife. My time is short and there is much to say." He stopped and struggled to breathe.

"Do not speak. There is no need. I know what is in your heart."

Demetrius ignored her words. "I have not thanked you enough for your love. You never gave up on me when others did. Your love gave me freedom and dignity. It is because of you that I am what I am. I thank you for your love, for the children you gave me, and for belief in one God."

"My darling, I would not be the woman I am without you. We loved each other, and God in His goodness joined us together."

Demetrius started to say something but a sudden bout of cough interrupted him.

"Don't speak, my love. Rest. A doctor will soon come. With God's help you will recover."

"I am dying my sweet and I don't need a doctor. I need you by my side."

"I will not leave you."

Demetrius was silent for a moment, then with a voice that could hardly be heard he said, "I have a request."

"Anything my love."

He labored for air and blood trickled from his mouth. His words came in gasps. It was with difficulty that he spoke. "Bosporus has been my adopted land which I love with all my heart. Here is where I gained my freedom, where I became a priest, where we were married, and where our children were born." He coughed and more blood came out of his mouth. Anastasia wiped his lips and pressed hers to his. With great effort he continued.

"But I am a Greek, and the land from which I was snatched is embedded in my heart." He stopped speaking and groaned in pain.

"Do not strain yourself. I know how much you love Greece."

With pleading eyes he looked at Anastasia and whispered, "Will you have a few grains of Greek soil brought to Bosporus, and sprinkle them on my grave? A little part of Greece will always be with me."

Anastasia squeezed his hand. With tears falling down her cheeks she murmured, "I will do as you ask, my sweet."

A priest came and gave him the Last Rites. Demetrius smiled. He was at peace, ready to enter the Kingdom of God. With sudden energy that comes to the dying, he lifted his arms and swung Anastasia to him. "Until I see you in heaven, my love." She remained in his arms until he breathed his last.

He was buried in the church graveyard with the whole congregation attending the funeral. Anastasia ordered soil from the Island of Crete to be shipped to Bosporus, and when it arrived she spread it over his grave. "Sleep well my darling until we meet again," she said.

And so Anastasia resumed her life as mother and minister of the Christian Church, serving all people who came to the church as well as those who didn't. The congregation in Bosporus grew and prospered, and hundreds were baptized. She lived a long and peaceful life, surrounded by the love and care of her children and grandchildren, and the people she served.

In her free moments she thought of her life as a girl in Rome, of her parents who loved her, especially her mother whom she came to admire and love dearly. She thought of her dear uncle who raised her, of Constantia whose generosity allowed her to live, and Odysseus whose act of kindness laid seeds of freedom for Bosporus' slaves.

And yes, there were moments when she thought of Valerius. He could have killed her and yet he let her live.

In his own way he loved her. Maybe in his last moments of life, he spoke to God and asked for forgiveness, and God forgave him, and made him a believer. She hoped it was so. She had forgiven him long ago, and felt no bitterness nor anger towards him, only sadness for a wasted life. A brilliant soldier, a talented man, he could have lived doing good. He chose the wrong path.

Dear to her heart was the Council of Nicaea and the Nicene Creed she prayed daily, and taught to her children. She felt privileged and humbled to have been a witness that established the Divinity and Equality of Jesus, as the Second Person of the Holy Trinity, the Only Begotten Son of the Father. What would have been her life had she not made the trip to Nicaea? She would never know and it didn't matter. Her short stay in Nicaea enriched her life. It exposed her to experiences available to very few, some good and some bad, but all invaluable in steering the fragile and unpredictable journey of life. She wouldn't change any part of it. Did she have regrets? Yes, a few. But they were eclipsed by the happiness and fulfillment of serving God with the man she loved.

When her time came to enter the Kingdom of God, her children and grandchildren prayed by her side, and all of Bosporus came to say farewell. She was a holy lady with a good heart, the people said. She did her part to make a better world, and was an example for generations to come.

They laid her by her husband in the church graveyard. The inscription read: *"Here lie Anastasia and Demetrius, wife and husband, ministers of the Christian Church, who worked faithfully and tirelessly for the good of the Church and God's people, whose love for Jesus Christ saw no bounds, and whose love for each other never wavered."*

THE END

CPSIA information can be obtained
at www.ICGtesting.com
Printed in the USA
LVHW100743110822
725714LV00010B/47

9 781478 739425